Here's what critics are saying about the Danger Cove Mysteries:

"High-octane entertainment and doesn't dip into a lull for even a sec! 5 stars!"
~ *Long Island Book Review*

"I am a frequent visitor to Danger Cove, and eager to stay for a long time. The mystery is very clever... put your inner Sherlock into high gear! Mixing it with some personal peril leads readers to a great conclusion...Loved it!"
~ *Kings River Life Magazine*

"The Danger Cove series continues to entertain as it showcases the talent of the GHP writers. This book is a keeper...I highly recommend this book!"
~ *Authors on the Air*

"One funny read! I started reading and was just sucked right in...a great mystery with twist and turns."
~ *Night Owl Reviews*

D1525120

DANGER COVE BOOKS

CLUES IN CALICO

a Danger Cove Mystery

Gin Jones &
Elizabeth Ashby

Thanks to Kathi again for so many things, but especially for helping me repurpose Keely's bank vault.

CHAPTER ONE

It could have been worse, I thought. *Much* worse.

I knew only too well how badly things could go wrong. I was an expert at anticipating worst-case scenarios. It had been an important part of my job as an attorney, and even after I'd had to change careers to reduce the stress in my life, I'd held onto the habit of always being prepared for any possible disaster.

Even with all my skill though, I hadn't anticipated just how much could go wrong while working as an appraiser of quilts. I'd always admired the artistry, so when I'd needed a new career, I'd thrown myself into the serious study of quilt history. Before long, I'd passed a rigorous exam that allowed me to put "certified quilt appraiser" underneath the "Keely Fairchild" on my business cards.

So what could possibly go wrong with my new career? In two words: Dee Madison.

Dee was president of the Danger Cove Quilt Guild. In her eighties, she definitely looked her age, with white hair, a fashion sense that was stuck in the 1980s, and a generally fragile appearance.

Dee might have been tiny, but when she declared something had to happen, there was no getting around her. Especially when her best friend and self-appointed enforcer, Emma Quinn, was nearby, which she always was. Emma was about ten years younger and several inches taller than Dee, although not quite my height. She had a sturdy build and a knack for organizing volunteers, even when said volunteers hadn't intended to step forward to help.

Apparently my certification as an appraiser wasn't enough. According to Dee—and therefore also according to Emma—I had to have hands-on experience with making quilts.

I liked Dee and Emma and respected their opinions, so about a month ago I'd given in to their pressure. Today was my first day as an active member of the guild, attending their regular Tuesday midday meeting.

Still, it could have been worse. I'd managed to convince them I could not and would not use the dangerous instrument commonly known as a sewing machine. Especially if it was one of the super-powered ones that Dee and Emma favored. In the course of my legal work, I'd seen the statistics on the dangers of motorized equipment, both large and small, and given my syncope diagnosis, I wasn't willing to take the chance that I'd pass out while my fingers were near a needle moving at the rate of five thousand stitches per minute. If I had to learn to quilt, it was going to be by hand, no electricity or motor required. After all, some of the most amazing quilts I'd ever seen, like the one made by Maria Dolores, the first keeper of the Danger Cove Lighthouse, had been sewn by hand, probably by the light of a kerosene lantern.

With the help of Dee and Emma, I'd settled on a single block that could be made into a nice little pillow rather than a huge bed covering. They'd guided me to a traditional Hawaiian design, a stylized breadfruit that had curved edges instead of the trickier-to-appliqué sharp points found in the more difficult patterns. I'd already cut the four connected leaves by folding a mottled turquoise fabric, tracing the pattern's design onto the top layer, and then cutting it as if I were making a paper snowflake. I'd even finished the next step all by myself: basting the turquoise fabric to the white background material.

According to the instructions, now I had to turn under the edges of the top fabric and stitch them to the background. In order to do that, I needed to consult with more experienced needle artists.

The Danger Cove Quilt Guild met in what had once been a gracious parlor in a Victorian-style house built in the early 1900s, a few buildings past Some Enchanted Florist and directly across from Pacific Heights Park. Over the years, it had been "rehabilitated" by removing all the interesting architectural elements. The fireplace had been covered over and the mantel removed, and the original plaster decoration on the ceiling had been replaced with a popcorn treatment.

I'd heard that Alex Jordan, the owner of Finials and Facades Renovation and Restoration Services had been thinking of buying the building. After seeing the ruined interior, she'd gone straight to one of her worksites and hammered things with far more force and relentlessness than required. It had taken well over an hour before she'd exhausted herself enough to let go of her outrage.

I hoped she hadn't seen what the current owner, a developer named Jack Condor, had been doing to the place in the past two years. Since the interior had already been stripped of its original elements, the historical commission had been helpless to prevent him from gutting the rooms in order to turn most of them into bland, modern medical office suites. At least the commission had been able to insist that the exterior be maintained in all its Painted Lady glory in keeping with the quaint, tourist-attracting nature of downtown Danger Cove.

Today, there were about a dozen women, one man, and a Labradoodle service dog in the first-floor room where the guild met. As the only part of the building that hadn't been gutted and renovated already, it had apparently been used as a staging area during the rest of the construction work. Scattered around were a few boxes of electrical outlets, a roll of industrial carpet, and several nail packs in a variety of sizes. Even the furniture appeared to be left over from earlier use, possibly abandoned by prior tenants. There wasn't much of it, just a collection of mismatched folding chairs, a metal desk, and two beat-up, laminate-topped banquet tables.

I'd no sooner entered the room than Dee and Emma came rushing over from where they'd been working in the strong natural light over by the bay window. We'd been friends for almost a year now, ever since they'd asked me for help with proving that a local quilt dealer was selling reproduction quilts as antiques, but I doubted they'd have been in such a hurry to leave their quilting projects if the only thing on their minds was to be gracious hostesses.

"You've got to talk to Jack Condor for us," Dee said as I braced myself. "He just told us that next week is the last time the guild can meet here. He finally got permission from the building department to turn this room into another office, and he's evicting us. You've got to stop it."

"It didn't work out so well the last time you asked me to talk to someone for you," I said. "The man ended up dead."

Dee opened her mouth, and I just knew she was going to say that the death was a perfectly acceptable result, in the case of both the shady quilt dealer and the guild's landlord, but Emma, even more accustomed than I was to her friend's sometimes thoughtless comments, spoke first.

"Randall Tremain's death wasn't our fault," Emma said. "Or yours, Keely. The man had been asking to be killed for years."

"That's true of Jack Condor too," Dee said irritably.

I hadn't met the man yet, but I'd heard all about him from Alex Jordan when I'd hired her to turn an abandoned bank building into my residence. Developers tended to have a bad reputation anyway, but this one lowered the bar even further. According to Alex, cheating and lying were Condor's stock in trade, and he had no respect for property or people. He wasn't from Danger Cove originally and didn't have any sentimental attachment to it, so he felt absolutely no compunctions about destroying the very things that made the town so special. The only local resident who might care if Condor died was Officer Fred Fields. Even then, it wasn't personal. It was just because Fred considered all crime—from murder all the way down to littering—to be an affront to his profession.

Even if I discounted some of what Alex had said about Condor as the exaggerations of a competitor, it was obvious that he wasn't a model citizen. He didn't even have the decency to give the guild a reasonable period of time to relocate, despite the guild's having met here every week since at least ten years before he'd bought the building. I might have been able to fight the eviction or at least delay it if I were still practicing law, but it wasn't an option now that I'd accepted my diagnosis of syncope, a not-very-well-understood condition characterized by an excessive response to stress, which included nausea, light-headedness, and sometimes even unconsciousness.

I was a quilt appraiser now, I reminded myself. And a novice quiltmaker. I didn't do anything the least bit stressful.

"Perhaps Jack Condor deserves whatever comes to him," Emma said, "but Keely is right about being careful in what we say and do. Now that the guild is being evicted, if anything happens to him, we'll be the prime suspects."

"I suppose that could be a problem." The wrinkles in Dee's face deepened while she thought. After a moment, she relaxed, and her eyes lit up. "Wait. I know. When Keely goes to talk to Condor, we won't go with her. We'll go somewhere public, with lots and lots of witnesses, so if anything happens to him, no one can blame us."

Right. They'd blame me. Just what I need in my search for a stress-free life.

"I'm not the right person to talk to your landlord." That was the truth, and not just because of my health issues. I didn't have much experience with landlord-tenant disputes. I'd always specialized in personal injury litigation. That was part of why I'd had to retire. There were some types of law where the risk of passing out with little notice wouldn't have been a major problem, but litigation wasn't one of them. Judges and juries tended to be a bit distracted by a lawyer who passed out in the middle of a closing argument.

"Lindsay says you can do anything you set your mind to," Dee said.

Bringing Lindsay Madison—Dee's granddaughter and my friend and ex-legal assistant—into the matter meant that I was going to lose the argument. I still felt a little guilty about having abandoned Lindsay when I quit the law office. She'd been on the verge of being fired by the managing partner at the time, and I hadn't been able to figure out how to get Lindsay to live up to her potential before I left. Since then, she'd improved on her own, but I still wished I'd been able to do more to help her.

If Dee called her granddaughter, Lindsay would drop everything at her job in Seattle and come back to Danger Cove to do whatever she could to help the guild. Including guilting me into doing a little bit of negotiating for the guild.

Some battles couldn't be won. I'd known as much in my trial practice, when the medical or forensic evidence hadn't been enough to support a claim. And I knew it now. I might have been a shark in pursuit of compensation for my clients, unswayed by both logical and emotional appeals, but I'd always had trouble saying no to people who needed my help.

"You don't need to bring your granddaughter into it," I said. "I'll make an appointment to talk to Jack Condor as soon as I leave here today."

If we'd been anywhere other than at a guild meeting, Dee would probably have insisted that I drop what I was doing and leave immediately to go see Condor. Quilting, however, came before anything else, including eating, sleeping, and business negotiations. As far as Dee was concerned, for some people quilting even came before breathing.

* * *

With the eviction resolved as far as Dee was concerned, she looked around the room for an appropriate tutor for my foray into appliqué. She shared a bit of silent communication with Emma, who then took me over to the table set up under the bay windows while Dee went over to chat with the sole male quilter and his service dog.

Emma introduced me to Faith Miller, probably the youngest woman in the room at no more than her early thirties. She was seated next to the head of the table with her back to the brilliant sunshine streaming in from the bay window. She was short and rounded with wispy blonde hair that stuck out in ways that seemed random, rather than an actual style, making her appear frazzled.

"It's so nice to meet you." Faith's voice was what I'd expect of a kindergarten teacher, all sweet and enthusiastic and as wispy as her hair. She even dressed like my image of a kindergarten teacher, in a mid-calf-length denim skirt and a V-neck knit shirt with crayon stains on one sleeve. "I've heard a lot about you."

I hoped it was in the context of quilt appraisals and not dead bodies.

"I'm glad to meet you too." I pointed at the stack of Robbing Peter to Pay Paul blocks on the table in front of her. It was a simple block, traditionally made with just two colors, alternating the placement of dark and light from block to block, so that when they were laid out, they formed an optical illusion of interlocking circles. While some quilters made the block on a sewing machine, Faith was using the alternate method of hand-appliquéing the curved pieces onto a background square. I couldn't imagine having the patience to make enough of them to cover an entire bed. "It looks like you've got a lot to teach me. I have a much smaller project, but I don't know where to start my stitching."

"Faith is a good teacher," Emma assured me. "She homeschools her three kids, in fact."

Faith smiled ruefully. "These Tuesday meetings are practically my only 'me' time. I trade with another homeschooler to have the afternoon off. Guild events are the only time I get to have any grown-up conversation. Don't get me wrong, I love my kids. But ever since my husband started traveling for several weeks at a time for his job, I'm practically a single parent. It gets to be too much sometimes, and if I don't get the occasional break from the kids and all the chores my husband used to do, I'm afraid I'm going to snap and do something I'd regret."

"I used to feel that way about my legal practice and my clients sometimes," I said. "I loved my work, but sometimes I needed a break. That's why I first started going to quilt shows."

Emma returned to the other end of the table where she'd left her current project, and I hung my quilted messenger bag on the back of the seat next to Faith at the head of the table before dropping into the chair. I placed the see-through, plastic quilter's version of the briefcase I'd once carried on the table. The brand new case held my basted breadfruit block, a packet of needles, and a spool of thread.

Faith examined my basting work and declared it to be passable. She was more enthusiastic about my choice of thread and needles, which I couldn't actually take any credit for, since they'd come in the kit with the pattern and fabric.

Faith demonstrated the needle-turn technique and the appliqué stitch on her own, more intricate block, and then, too soon in my estimation, it was time for me to take my own first stitches at the point she suggested in the center of the design.

Faith had made it look easy, using her needle to turn under the raw edge of the turquoise fabric and then taking invisible stitches every sixteenth of an inch.

My first stitch looked like an errant eyebrow in need of plucking.

"Don't worry," Faith said in her sweet, encouraging voice. "Just keep going, and it will get easier. Then you can pull out these first stitches and redo them if you want."

She was the expert, chosen by meta-experts, so I had to trust her.

The next stitch wasn't quite so obviously a mess, and the next one almost looked like the worst of Faith's.

Almost.

Faith glanced at my work. "If you need help after the meeting, you can always call me. I don't answer if I'm too busy, which seems like all the time now. But I do love talking about quilts. And the chance to have a grown-up conversation. You probably won't need any help, though. It's really just a matter of practice."

"Thanks." I gave her one of my business cards so she could send me her contact information.

Trusting that Faith was right that repetition would improve my needlework, I returned to my stitching. I'd completed perhaps a dozen of what looked to be thousands of stitches in just that one pillow-sized block when I heard the outer door slam shut.

A moment later, a scruffy, scrawny, middle-aged man appeared in the doorway of the parlor. He wore faded jeans that looked like they'd seen years of wear, rather than being artificially aged by the manufacturer. His plaid flannel shirt was unbuttoned, revealing a dingy white t-shirt with food stains all down the front.

The man hesitated in the doorway, clearly ill at ease. I'd seen that sort of look on other men entering a room full of women and finding this kind of male-to-female ratio intimidating. His gaze finally settled on the one male in the room, and his eyes lit with relief. He started for the table where the male quilter was working, but Emma got to the newcomer before he'd taken more than a few steps.

"Hello," she said, taking his reluctant hand in hers for a sturdy shake. "I'm Emma Quinn. Are you here to join the quilt guild?"

"Um, not exactly," he said. "I was hoping to talk to someone who knows about quilt pricing. See, my cousin died, and she was a quilter, and now I've got to figure out what to do with her stuff. I found a flyer about the guild when I was looking for her will. I thought maybe someone here could help me figure out what the quilts are worth and how I can sell them."

To a woman—and man and Labradoodle—everyone turned to look at me.

Emma took the newcomer by the elbow and headed in my direction. "You must be related to Miriam Stafford."

Beside me, Faith gasped and then whispered, "I didn't know Miriam had died."

The man was nodding. "Herb Stafford."

"We're all so sorry for your loss," Emma said. "Miriam was a dedicated quiltmaker and far too young to have completed all the quilts she was capable of. Her death was such a loss for the guild."

Herb nodded, his feet dragging a bit as Emma pulled him deeper into the room full of women.

Emma either didn't notice his reluctance or didn't care about it. "I know just who you need to talk to. Keely Fairchild. She's a certified quilt appraiser. You're in luck, because she's here today, so you can schedule an appointment right away."

Herb stopped dragging his feet. "That's good. It's already been three weeks since Miriam passed, and I need to get the information together as soon as possible for my attorney to start the process. It's already been delayed a bit since I had to search for the will."

I put down my needlework, somewhat relieved by the interruption. It was going to take far more than the number of stitches I could do during this meeting before I got the hang of this new skill. Assuming I ever did. Not everyone had good eye-hand coordination, after all, and I'd never really tried anything that required that particular skill, so I might be a total klutz. Worse, I might be one of those people who were so bad at an activity that they couldn't even recognize how bad they were and flaunted their horrible handiwork. Instead of using my hands-on quiltmaking to buttress my credentials as an appraiser, my poor stitching would undermine my expertise.

I pulled out the seat across from Faith and gestured for Herb to sit beside me.

As he approached, Faith began to cough and wave a hand in front of her face as if trying to fan away noxious fumes. I didn't have a particularly keen sense of smell, but even I couldn't miss the smell of the cigarette smoke that seemed to be steeped into the fibers of his clothing.

Faith bundled up her work as if it were one of her children being exposed to noxious fumes, and scurried off, leaving me and Herb isolated at one end of the table.

"Thank you," he said. "Ms. Fairchild, was it?"

"Keely." I dug in my messenger bag for another business card and handed it to him. "Tell me a bit about your cousin's quilts."

"I don't know much." He adjusted the placement of the chair next to me and settled into it. "I just know she's got lots of them, and it's up to me to figure out what to do with them all. I'm the only one left in our family, I'm afraid."

"I'd be glad to take a preliminary look at the quilts to see whether they're worth doing in-depth appraisals."

"Oh, I'm sure they are," Herb said. "She's been selling them online, supporting herself nicely for almost ten years now."

"Let me check my schedule." I scrolled through the calendar on my smartphone. Business had really been picking up, both through the Danger Cove Historical Museum's new acquisition program and assorted referrals to private collectors. Still, it wasn't like when I was a trial lawyer and every minute of my day, stretching out for the next six months, was fully booked. I had to finish up a major project for the museum in the next few days, but after that my schedule was fairly light. "How about Monday? I could spend as much time with the quilts as you need then."

"Nothing sooner?" he said. "It's just that I'd really like to be able to give the attorney a rough idea of what the quilts are worth. She said she needed an estimate—even a guesstimate is fine, but I can't even do that much myself—in order to file the preliminary paperwork."

I wasn't in any real rush to finish my appliqué block, and Dee would understand if I left the guild meeting early to do something related to quilting, especially since it would also give me the chance to make an appointment with Jack Condor. "The only unscheduled time I have this week is in the next couple of hours. I couldn't do anything major in that timeframe, but I could at least get an idea of the scope of the project and let you know what I would charge if you decide to hire me."

Herb jumped to his feet. "That would be perfect. I'll text the address to the phone number on your card."

"I need a few minutes to wrap up what I'm doing here," I said. "Why don't I meet you there in half an hour?"

Herb gave me his phone number to add to my contacts list before he left. I had to force myself to move slowly and not haphazardly stuff my fabric and other supplies into the carrying case. It wouldn't be good for my reputation if I looked as pleased as I felt about having an excuse to skip out early on my first lesson in quiltmaking.

CHAPTER TWO

I'd almost finished the intentionally slow packing of my supplies when I noticed Faith hadn't resumed her work since we'd been interrupted by Herb's arrival. She seemed frozen in her new seat, staring unseeing at her hands.

I slung my messenger bag's strap over my shoulder and carried my supplies over to check on her. "I'm sorry. Was Miriam a friend of yours?"

Faith started and then laughed nervously. "Not exactly. I do try not to judge, lest I be judged. I knew she was an unhappy person, and not in the best of health, so I should have been more understanding. It's just that...no, I don't want to speak ill of the dead, so I'll just say we never did get along."

Then why was Faith so upset about Miriam's death?

I didn't have time to do a thorough cross-examination, but I was curious, and I didn't think it would take much to encourage Faith to confide what she hadn't liked about Miriam. Taking depositions of witnesses had taught me that sometimes people just needed to be given a chance to unburden themselves. A sympathetic look, a vague bit of commiseration, and it would all come pouring out.

I dragged out the process of packing the last supplies into my case, checking that everything was neatly folded or wrapped and then moving pieces from one spot to another as if concerned that they weren't in exactly the right location.

Faith suddenly dove into the canvas beach bag beside her chair, rummaging for something. "I wouldn't say anything normally, but you're an appraiser. You understand these things. And you need to know what to watch out for when Miriam's quilts hit the market."

She handed me her phone with the home screen featuring the picture of a stunning Robbing Peter to Pay Paul quilt. It was made from a wide variety of prints in cool blues, purples, and silvers, and the placement of the darks and lights created a secondary design, like a brainteaser puzzle that had one obvious image plus another one that was only visible when it was viewed from the right angle.

"That's lovely," I said as I handed back the phone. If I were appraising it, I'd add some extra value because of the unusual layout.

"Thank you. I love the Robbing Peter block. There's so much you can do with it, just by changing the layout and color choices. I made this version for last year's guild show." Faith scrolled through some other pictures on her phone until she found the one she wanted and showed it to me. "Compare that to the quilt Miriam brought to show-and-tell about a month ago. She said she'd just finished it that week. Almost a full year after mine was in the show."

The picture was of another Robbing Peter to Pay Paul quilt, smaller than Faith's, I thought, but still bed-sized. It was also a scrappy quilt, with each piece a different color and print, and laid out in much the same way as Faith's to create a secondary design. The biggest difference was in the color palette, a collection of warm oranges, browns, and yellows instead of Faith's cooler blues. Adjusting for the color differences, it still wasn't an exact match, but it was definitely similar. Enough that, if I were appraising them, I'd have wondered if the second one had been made by the same quilter or at least by someone who'd been influenced by the first one.

I wasn't sure what Faith's point was, so I just nodded my head appreciatively and waited for her to continue.

"I know that imitation is supposed to be the sincerest form of flattery," she said, "but when I saw Miriam's quilt for sale online, it didn't feel at all flattering. I wanted to have a tantrum to rival my youngest child's. I gave myself a time-out to think about how to respond, but now she's dead, and I'll never get the satisfaction of hearing her admit, in front of the entire guild, what she did."

Faith took back her picture and phone. "I suppose I need to forgive her and move on now. It may be a while, though, before I can pray for her soul. I'm not as good a person as I'd like to be."

"None of us are," I said. "We just try to do our best."

Faith sighed. "I wish it weren't always so hard to do the right thing. Fortunately, I've always believed in turning the other cheek, rather than taking revenge. Seeing my design stolen by someone who was supposed to be a friend definitely made me feel like I'd been stabbed in the back. I'll even admit to briefly wanting to do the same thing to Miriam. Literally, and not metaphorically."

I assured Faith that, in my experience, everyone felt that sort of anger occasionally, and the important thing was that she hadn't acted on her urges. She didn't look convinced, but I was running out of time if I were going to arrive on time to check out Miriam's quilt collection.

* * *

I'd given up driving as soon as I was diagnosed with syncope. The risk of passing out behind the wheel wasn't one I was willing to take. Not having a car wasn't usually a problem in Danger Cove, since I lived near the center of town and could walk to most of the places I needed to go. For slightly longer distances, I could always hop on the trolley that connected Main Street and the waterfront, and for anything else I could call a cab.

The street where Miriam had lived was within easy walking distance of where the guild met, in the opposite direction from Some Enchanted Florist. Her house was near the turn-around at the far end of a quiet cul-de-sac lined with well-maintained little homes that had all the necessities for a residence, but no architectural frills. They had little, white picket fences separating their lots, and many of them were small ranches, including Miriam's and the houses on either side of hers. All of the structures on the street had probably been virtually identical originally, built by a single developer—one who was not as disliked as Jack Condor, I hoped—in the middle of the twentieth century, but some of them had been added onto in the meantime. The one to the left of Miriam's was a dark green that almost disappeared behind the profusion of flowers in the front yard, which had been turned into one massive English garden. The beige house to the right was less eye-catching, with a more conventional landscaping. Still, it was in pristine condition, presumably at least partly to maintain the curb appeal while there was a *For Sale* sign in the front yard.

Miriam's house looked less pristine than her immediate neighbors' homes. At first, I thought her siding was a badly weathered shade of red, but as I went through the front gate and up the walkway, I could tell that it had been painted within the last few years, far too recently for the color to be anything but a close approximation of the intended hue. It was as if the usual proportions of dominant color and accents had been reversed, with the siding an intense pumpkin orange more usually seen in the smaller elements of a house, and the trim the same sedate beige as the siding on the house to the right.

Of course, the owner of the rust-colored house had been a quiltmaker, and one of the things I'd always admired about quilts, beginning long before I was certified as an appraiser, was the sometimes adventurous use of color.

Herb Stafford was waiting for me on the front porch. He stubbed out his cigarette on the concrete steps and tossed the butt into the shrubbery. He'd left the door open while he was outside, so he stepped aside with a gesture for me to precede him into the living room.

Inside, dominating the entire space and facing the picture window at the front of the house, was a professional setup for machine stitching the layers of a quilt together. The only other furniture in the room was a leather recliner against the side wall. Not counting the quilts in the room, the overall effect was Spartan, without any rugs on the wood floors or even curtains on the window, which seemed odd for someone who appreciated textiles as much as Miriam purportedly did.

A king-sized quilt top, layered with batting and backing, had been stretched onto the rails of the quilting setup. The arm of an oversized sewing machine arched over the quilt, ready to pick up where Miriam had last left off. While I couldn't see the mechanics of it from the door, I knew that the sewing machine was affixed to a rolling base, which allowed for the arm to be moved across the plane of the quilt by the operator, using handles affixed above where the needle pierced the quilt.

The quilt design was known as the Variable Star. The pieced blocks consisted of indigo stars on a white background, and they alternated with unpieced squares in an orange that was similar to the exterior of the house. Experts referred to the color as antimony or chrome orange; everyone else called it "cheddar." It wasn't as popular today as it had been in the late 1800s, but it still had a devoted group of collectors and creators.

Miriam had obviously been a huge fan of cheddar quilts. In addition to the one on the frame and the one that Faith had claimed was a copy of her design, there was a small antique cheddar quilt, framed and hung on an interior wall to the right of the door. The antique was yet another Robbing Peter to Pay Paul design, but in a much simpler layout than Faith's. The individual fabrics were more interesting than the design, with historic cheddar prints alternating with traditional "shirtings," tiny prints on a pale background.

It was just a guess, but I thought the antique might have been a salvaged section from a much larger quilt that had been damaged beyond repair. The remaining section was only about two feet wide by three feet high, with edge blocks that were seemingly random widths, rather than full or half blocks. On closer inspection, the binding, while made of old shirtings, was suspiciously pristine, with fewer stains than the rest of the quilt and without the wear and tear that the edges of an antique textile usually experienced.

The quilt fragment had been professionally framed, with appropriate spacers to prevent the accumulation of moisture. Ideally, a quilt of that age should have had even greater protection from sunlight, although at least it wasn't subjected to direct light. The large picture windows faced north, limiting how much sunlight fell on either the contemporary quilt in the machine's frame or the antique on the wall.

There must have been twenty other quilts in the room. The patterns varied, but almost all of the quilts included at least some cheddar orange fabrics. Miriam wasn't the most organized person, though. Her quilts weren't folded and stacked or—better yet—laid out on a flat surface as I would have recommended to minimize wear and tear. Instead, they were strewn around the room, three of them hanging off the rails of the machine-quilting setup, others balled up and tossed aside, and the rest scrunched up on the recliner.

Herb must have noticed my bemusement, because he said, "Sorry about the mess. You can see why I couldn't stay here while I'm working on Miriam's estate. I had to get a room at the Ocean View B&B. The police only released the scene a few days ago, and I've been so busy looking for Miriam's will since then that I haven't had a chance to straighten up. She was an immaculate housekeeper and would have been appalled to know anyone saw the place like this."

I hadn't agreed to get involved with anything as stressful as a crime scene. "Why were the police involved?"

"Didn't you know?" he said. "Poor Miriam was murdered. Whoever killed her tossed the place."

* * *

I should have known better than to think this was going to be easy. I'd been looking forward to a quick rummage through her collection, just enough to determine whether they were worth in-depth appraisals. I was assuming Miriam had the typical dozen or so quilts, none of them antique or even vintage, with a cumulative value in the range of five to ten thousand dollars. If I was right, then individual appraisals would cost almost as much as each quilt was worth, so all that Herb was likely to do was hire me to give him and his attorney an informal ballpark figure for the entire collection. In that case, I could be done here in less than half an hour.

It was just as well. I had plenty of other work that needed to be completed this week, like finishing the report on a collection of vintage quilts the Danger Cove Historical Museum was considering acquiring. And I couldn't forget my latest high-priority project: convincing Jack Condor to reconsider his eviction of the quilt guild.

"I'm sorry," Herb said. "I thought you knew. It looks like her killer was looking for something. I think he knew she was wealthier than her house and personal appearance might suggest, and he was looking for money. Apparently he didn't know that the quilts he was tossing aside were the sole source of her wealth, or he'd have taken them with him."

So far I hadn't noticed anything that suggested Miriam's quilts were particularly valuable in anything but sentimental terms. They were all contemporary and featured fairly simple, traditional patterns. The workmanship was solid, but the designs weren't anything out of the ordinary, nothing as complicated as Faith's Robbing Peter to Pay Paul.

Unless I'd missed something that only a closer inspection would reveal, the odds were that each of the quilts would only sell for between three and five hundred dollars. Even that was a generous evaluation. The total would be a nice sum, given the number of the quilts in the room, but it would require months of work by a knowledgeable seller with contacts in the quilt-collecting community to get that much for them. Otherwise, they could bring in as little as a hundred dollars apiece.

Perhaps there was more to Miriam's collection, though, since Herb was so obviously convinced it was valuable. She might have kept her more valuable quilts in another room. "Are there any other quilts in the house besides these?"

"Oh, yes," Herb said. "This is just where Miriam did the machine quilting and stored the most recently finished quilts before she had time to list them for sale online. All the rest are in the second bedroom. She turned it into her sewing room. Her fabric and supplies are in there too. In fact, they're probably worth quite a bit as well. I know she complained about how much she had to pay for quilting thread in hard-to-find colors."

I followed him down the short hallway to get a quick look at the rest of the collection. The sewing room was dominated by cheddar orange. There were at least ten full bolts of fabric leaning against the wall across from the door, half of them orange prints and the other half orange solids. Lined up as they were, from darkest to lightest, they looked like an experiment in dyeing gradations.

Another wall had floor-to-ceiling built-in cubbies, the bulk of them filled with folded fabric and spools of thread, all sorted by color, much of it in the warmer end of the spectrum.

The very top row was packed with books about quilts, some of them focused on patterns and others containing a mix of photographs and historical information.

I could only dream of having that many reference books for my collection, some of them rare enough to make it worth the effort for the estate to look for a buyer who would pay a decent price rather than donating them to Goodwill. The new owner of the local bookstore, Dangerous Reads, might be willing to buy the whole collection or else arrange some sort of consignment deal with the estate.

The third wall was covered with two giant, flannel-covered design boards that ran from the floor to a few inches from the ceiling. The one closer to the door displayed the first few blocks for yet another cheddar quilt and the other had what appeared to be leftover blocks from a previous project. The remaining wall was dominated by a custom worktable. At one end was a sewing machine dropped into an opening so the machine bed was level with the surface of the table. At the other end, another cutout was filled with a three-foot by four-foot ironing surface. Stuffed underneath, filling every bit of space except for where the rolling chair was neatly tucked under the sewing machine, were cylinders of rolled batting in a variety of colors and sizes.

"Check this out," Herb said, heading for the nearest flannel-covered design board. "There's a hidden compartment behind the design wall, and that's where Miriam kept the finished quilts that hadn't sold yet. The killer must not have known about it, because as far as I can tell, it hasn't been touched."

He slid the first design board along a hidden track until it was in front of the second board. In the space behind them was shelf after shelf of neatly folded quilts with little tags that reminded me of the ones antique-quilt dealer Randall Tremain had attached to his inventory at his shop, Monograms. Except for a few relegated to obscurity on a hard-to-reach top shelf in the far corner, most of the quilts featured the cheddar prints that Miriam favored.

"There must be more than a hundred quilts in there."

"I could tell you exactly how many if the police would let me have her computer back with all of its inventory information," Herb said. "Although, I might need some help from someone who understands her software. She was always much better with numbers than I am."

"Just inventorying these quilts would take several days," I said. "Doing complete appraisals on all of them would take weeks, and I don't have that much time open in my schedule. Are you sure you really need that much information for your attorney?"

"I don't need an in-depth appraisal right now," Herb said. "The lawyer said she just needed a ballpark figure for the entire collection in order to get things started in the probate court. Then we can talk about more in-depth inventorying and valuation."

"It would have to be a very rough ballpark," I said. "I can tell you the average of prices for contemporary quilts, and you can multiply that by the number of quilts. I might be able to do more in-depth work next week, at least enough to let you know which ones are more valuable than the others, if not to do full appraisals."

"That would help a lot." He slid the flannel-covered board back to its original location and turned to me expectantly. "So, what do you think? A thousand dollars apiece? Five? More?"

"Quilts tend to be under-valued in the marketplace." I braced myself for what could be a bad response to unwanted news. It should be easier to break the news to someone who hadn't invested hundreds of hours creating something that would return about ten cents an hour to its maker. Still, it was going to be a challenge, since Herb's expectations were so far out of line with reality. "I've seen estimates that handmade quilts at craft shows sell for anywhere between $200 and $500, depending on their size."

He frowned. "That can't be right. I know Miriam made a good living selling her quilts online. Paid off the mortgage on this house several years ago, even. She certainly didn't have any retirement income, not after working her entire career for old Miser Dreiser. She was always complaining about how he underpaid her and wouldn't even set up a company-sponsored retirement plan for her, let alone contribute a single penny to it. He didn't even give her any severance pay when he fired her."

I'd never been terribly good at soothing emotional clients, and I didn't have much time available today. I needed to visit the museum's archives to finish another project and also make sure to contact Jack Condor before the end of business hours. Dee might accept that I couldn't meet with the guild's landlord today, but if I wanted to keep her from getting her granddaughter involved, I had to at least be able to tell her I'd scheduled an appointment.

"I'd be glad to provide you with the names and contact information for other appraisers to get a second opinion," I said. "Or you could check the websites of the American Quilter's Society or the Professional Association of Appraisers—Quilted Textiles. They've both got search tools for finding a qualified appraiser."

"I'll do that." Herb stalked out of the room in an obvious hint that it was time for me to leave. The smell of cigarettes trailed after him, and his voice drifted back from the hallway. "It's obvious that you aren't qualified to do the work with Miriam's quilts."

CHAPTER THREE

———

I was far more relieved than offended that Herb didn't want to hire me. If a prospective client was going to be more trouble to work with than he was worth, it was always best to find out before the contract was signed. Especially now that stress wasn't a distant concept, something that I knew in theory was bad for me but could ignore for the most part.

I followed Herb out of the house instead of lingering in Miriam's work room. Normally, I would have been intrigued by the opportunity to take a closer look at her unusual quilt collection but not if it meant working with a difficult client.

Fortunately, I had plenty of paid work to do for a much more pleasant client. A local pair of elderly sisters had offered to donate some of their quilts to the Danger Cove Historical Museum, and I'd been asked to see which of them might fit in best with the rest of the museum's collection. I'd narrowed the possibilities down to five, and I needed to do some research in the museum's archives before making a final recommendation.

The walk to the museum would be good for me, relieving what little irritation remained from my experience with Herb. Besides, we'd had a colder and longer winter than usual, with pleasant spring weather arriving only now, the last week of April. Today's sunny weather was perfect for walking.

Leaving the cul-de-sac, I turned left as if I were returning to where the quilt guild met. The sight of the building reminded me that I needed to call Jack Condor's office. Blocking out the sound of the kids playing across the street in Pacific Heights Park, I managed to schedule an appointment to talk to the guild's landlord for the next day.

By then, I'd reached Some Enchanted Florist. My doctor was always telling me to slow down, to stop and smell the roses, so I paused to look in the window and admire the sample arrangements. The bunnies and eggs of Easter had been packed away, and now the shop was promoting tulips with arrangements that turned even the simplest, traditional variety into something spectacular. The owner, George Fontaine, wasn't just a dashing man of mystery—I'd heard quite a few rumors, and no concrete answers, about his adventurous life before moving to Danger Cove and purchasing the florist shop—he was also as much of an artist with his medium as the quilters were with theirs.

Unfortunately, even though my fledgling appraisal business was doing better than expected, my budget was too tight to indulge in a floral arrangement today when I didn't have any particular reason to celebrate other than successfully avoiding getting dragged into yet another homicide investigation. Depending on who was investigating Miriam's death, the mere fact that I had been invited to the victim's house would either get me condescended to—that would be Detective Lester Marshall—or sternly warned to leave the investigating to the professionals—that would be Detective Bud Ohlsen.

I continued to Main Street and then across to where the aromas emanating from Cinnamon Sugar Bakery reminded me that my budget *did* extend to a mid-afternoon snack.

After a quick stop for a lemon poppy-seed cupcake, I arrived at the museum. I called out a greeting to Liz—she'd never told me her last name—the elderly woman who sold tickets at the front desk. She lowered her e-reader from where she held it about three inches from her eyes and waved me toward the central stairs before returning to her book. As a frequent visitor, I had a permanent pass to the museum and an electronic key to the archives.

At the top of the stairs, I'd intended to turn down the corridor toward the archives, but I happened to catch sight of Gil—short for Gillian, but pronounced with a hard G—Torres coming out of her suite at the opposite end of the corridor.

It would have been impossible not to notice her. I'm tall, but Gil, at a hair under six feet, was three inches taller than me in flats, and today she was wearing high-heeled sandals in keeping with the belated arrival of warm spring weather. Her overall look was always professional, but with a flair that I would never achieve. My navy cardigan, light-blue knit shirt and skinny jeans were more casual than my previous wardrobe of jury-trial-appropriate suits, but they would never turn heads like Gil's intricately quilted red jacket and stark black trousers would.

She called out my name. "I'm so glad you're here." Gil sang a bit of Three Dog Night's "Joy to the World" as she headed in my direction. "If you've got a minute, I need to talk to you about a major project that just fell into my lap."

"I've always got time for you." I turned toward her office. "How can I help?"

"I have to warn you, it could be time-consuming."

The museum was my biggest single client, and a new project would go a long way toward distracting me from thoughts of what I'd missed by not getting a more thorough look at Miriam's quilt collection. "As long as it doesn't involve me going to court or doing anything stressful, I'll find the time."

Gil unlocked her inner office and went around the desk. "We're already working with an attorney, and it just involves inventorying a quilt collection. Some people might find that stressful, but not you."

"Sounds like fun." I settled into one of the guest chairs. "What's the scope of the project?"

"I'm not entirely sure yet," Gil said. "We just got a call from Aaron Pohoke. I don't know if you've met him yet, but he's an attorney here in town, and he was just appointed the personal representative of the estate of a quilter. Apparently, she had an extensive collection of quilts, and they were bequeathed to the museum."

"Let me guess," I said. "Miriam Stafford."

Gil nodded. "The quilters' grapevine is even better than I thought."

"Just a fluke this time. Miriam's cousin was thinking of hiring me to appraise the quilts, so I was just at her house to discuss his options with him. As it turned out, he didn't like anything I had to offer." Now I was even more relieved that I hadn't agreed to work for him. If the museum hired me, I could enjoy viewing Miriam's quilts without having to deal with Herb's unreasonable expectations. "Are you absolutely sure the will names the museum? Her cousin seems to think he's the sole heir."

"I should have known it was too good to be true," Gil said, drawing out the last five words in a bluesy wail. "I've heard what can happen if there's a will contest. Even if the museum wins and doesn't spend more on legal fees than the inheritance is worth, there's always some negative PR with the loser claiming that the museum is stealing their family memories."

"The publicity is likely to be particularly persistent in this case," I said. "Miriam didn't die of natural causes, and they haven't identified the killer."

Gil groaned. "The museum doesn't need to be associated with any more sordid events."

"I'm afraid there's nothing much you can do about it now. Until the homicide case is closed, the story, complete with references to the museum's inheritance, will keep popping back up in the news every time you think people have forgotten about it."

"I'll have to talk to Aaron again," Gil said. "He told me the woman died three weeks ago, but he didn't say anything about murder. He just apologized for taking so long to let us know about the will. He'd been tied up in a trial for a week after Miriam died, and he didn't hear about it until a few days ago. He said I'd get an official notice in a few days along with a copy of the will, but for now he just wanted to let me know that the museum will be getting a bunch of quilts. Aaron's also been trying to get in touch with the other heir, Miriam's cousin, but he didn't have a phone number for him."

"I do." I scrolled through the contacts on my phone and then read out the number to Gil. "If that doesn't work, Herb mentioned he was staying at the Ocean View B&B, so the attorney could leave a message there. I'm sure Bree Milford would make sure Herb got it."

"I'll let Aaron know." Gil keyed a note into her laptop. "I'm probably going to regret asking this because it would probably be better if I didn't get too excited about the inheritance before I'm sure it will happen, but did you see Miriam's collection? I'm told it's unique."

"It is," I said. "But not necessarily in a valuable way. It's just a guess, but I'd say there are at least a hundred fifty quilts in her house, and most of them are modern cheddar quilts. Orange isn't a terribly popular color today, which might negatively affect the value, but I'm sure there are some collectors who might be interested in buying them. There was also one antique Robbing Peter to Pay Paul, but it was just a fragment. I'd need to take a closer look and do some research to give you any more details on it."

"Regardless of the value, we'll need to get an accurate count and make some decisions about which ones are worth keeping and which should be sold," Gil said. "Aaron said he'd leave that up to us, since he certainly doesn't have the expertise to do it. Assuming he's confident that the will is valid and that it's worth going forward, do you have time to do an inventory of the quilts?"

"I'll put together a proposal for the work and have it to you tonight," I said. "I'm almost done with the work on the Bergman sisters' quilts, so I should be able to focus on this project next."

"The sooner, the better," Gil said. "The museum's board meeting is a week from tomorrow, and I'd like to have at least preliminary information on the quilts to share with them."

"In that case, I'd better get home to write the proposal." I stood, slinging my messenger bag over my shoulder. "Before I go, there is something else I wanted to talk to you about. I don't know if you've heard yet, but the quilt guild is being evicted from their meeting space, and they're looking for a new one. I know they do some of their special events here in the boardroom. Is there a reason why they don't have their regular meetings there too?"

"We've never really talked about it. As far as I knew, they were happy in their current location. I'll ask the board if they'll consider offering the guild a permanent reservation, but in the past they've resisted doing that for anyone. They even turned down the Save the Lighthouse committee, which really annoyed me. The boardroom is supposed to be available for community events, after all. I'd be happy to see it get more use, but I don't have the authority to do long-term bookings. I can only authorize the use of the room for a single month without board approval. Then the guild would have to reapply, and if some other group happened to get the paperwork in before them, I can't play favorites, so I'd have to turn down the guild."

"The quilters need more stability than you can offer," I said. "If you could set aside the next few Tuesdays and Saturdays for the guild though, that would buy us some time to look for a more permanent location."

"Unfortunately, I'm pretty sure it's not available the next few Saturdays. A writers group has booked one for a workshop with Elizabeth Ashby and the Farmers' Market's manager has two others to meet with the vendors. Normally, Tuesdays are less busy, but the Garden Club might have claimed at least one of them. I'll check and let you know. And in the meantime, I'll talk to the board again about a longer arrangement, if you want. The news about the quilts we're inheriting—assuming that goes smoothly—might make them more receptive to the idea of the guild meeting here."

"I'd appreciate it." I adjusted the strap on my messenger bag. "Dee thinks I'm going to convince Jack Condor to let them stay in their current space, and I'll do my best, but I'd feel a lot better if I knew there was a backup plan."

"Just don't count on the board agreeing to the long-term commitment," Gil said. "I always have the best plans going into a board meeting, but afterwards it seems like I never get to say, 'I love it when a plan comes together.'"

* * *

It took much less time than I'd expected to find exactly what I needed in the archives. I could finish my report on the Bergman sisters' quilts in the evening, a couple of days ahead of schedule. Then I'd be free to start in on Miriam's collection.

On my way out, I saw my favorite reporter, Matt Viera, in the lobby, chatting with the ticket-taker at her desk. Liz was close to ninety years old, white-haired, practically deaf and blind, despite her hearing aids and glasses, and yet she was every bit as susceptible to Matt's charm as every other woman who'd ever caught a glimpse of him. Including me.

Matt was tall and lean with dark hair and the sort of sharply defined facial features that made him extremely photogenic. He didn't pay much attention to his appearance though, so his hair was always a bit past due for a trim, and he dressed casually in cargo pants he'd acquired during his previous career as a fashion model. They had about twice as many pockets as standard, and he usually wore them with a sport shirt, also probably left over from a photo shoot. Today's shirt was a faded purple, too dark to be pastel, but too muddy to be called "grape." It reminded me of some of the truly ugly fabrics that I'd seen quilters swoon over. Apparently they were prized for use in scrap quilts since they provided a contrast to the prettier prints and a place for the eye to rest amidst the chaos of the many other exciting fabrics. Even so, I thought the color of Matt's shirt would have been a challenge for quilters to use, even if it were cut into the tiniest of pieces.

And yet somehow, he made it look trendy.

Matt must have heard my footsteps because he patted Liz's hand in farewell and turned to face me. "Well, if it isn't my favorite lawyer-turned-quilter."

"I wouldn't say I'm a quilter," I said. "I'm making a pillow. Maybe."

Matt shrugged. "It's like any addiction. You start with just a taste, and then it turns into an irresistible craving."

"Dee and Emma don't exactly fit the image of drug pushers."

"Sure they do," Matt said. "They're persistent, and they make it hard to say no to them."

He had a point. Dee didn't hear the word "no," and Emma simply steam-rolled over it.

A mother and three preteen kids came in the front door and headed over to get her tickets, reminding me that Matt and I weren't alone. It probably wouldn't be good for the museum's reputation if visitors overheard a conversation about addiction. Gil was having enough trouble reassuring potential visitors that the murder that had happened in the back parking lot shortly before Christmas was just a fluke and not an indication that the place was unsafe.

"We should probably go somewhere private to continue our conversation."

Matt waggled his eyebrows. "I thought you'd never ask. How about your vault?"

When I'd had the bank building renovated into my residence, I'd left the vault in place, since the cost to remove it would have been exorbitant. Matt had been asking to see it ever since I first met him, but initially I hadn't trusted him, and then once I'd gotten to know him better, we'd had conflicting schedules.

The last couple of months, the conflicts had been more of my own devising than real. I kept waffling over how much I wanted him to know about me. I'd always had to be careful about what people knew about me personally, because image and reputation were critical to my career as a trial lawyer. It was different now, but old habits died hard.

The way I'd converted the vault wasn't as personal as, for instance, my syncope diagnosis, which I'd only shared with my very closest friends. Still, the interior of the vault would reveal things about me that I wouldn't have wanted my fellow attorneys to know back when I was still practicing, because it would have negatively affected their image of me. I no longer cared about what they thought, but I was starting to care about how Matt would react to seeing the real me. His response to the contents of the vault would be a useful indicator of whether it was safe to tell him about my health issues. I'd seen how badly some of my friends had taken the diagnosis, and I wasn't looking forward to seeing Matt look at me with that sad, pitying expression.

I'd promised to show him the vault, and I would, but at the moment, the timing was wrong. I had too much work to do between inventorying Miriam's quilt collection and finding a new meeting space for the guild. I couldn't risk any increased demands on my nervous system right now.

"The vault's a mess at the moment," I said. "Do you mind waiting until after I get a chance to do some spring cleaning?"

Matt held my gaze for what seemed like forever, and I was pretty sure he knew I was just procrastinating.

Eventually he shrugged and headed across the lobby to the main door. "I've waited this long—a little more time won't kill me. But you need to make it up to me. I need a favor from you. I was just on my way to see Gil about the museum's inheritance from Miriam Stafford. It would make a great story, and it's been a while since there's been anything happening right here in Danger Cove that was both arts-related and worth writing about."

"Word really does get around fast," I said as I walked with him.

He gave me a wounded look. "Hey, I am a reporter."

"Arts and entertainment reporter," I corrected. "I wouldn't expect you to be hanging out at the court, reading the filings there."

"I don't." Matt held the front door for me. "One of my colleagues, Duncan Pickles, was keeping an eye out for the filing of Miriam's will as part of his coverage of her death. It's been about three weeks now, and as far as anyone knows, the police don't have any solid leads. Duncan read the will and tipped me off to the museum's inheritance. I tried to talk to Aaron Pohoke—he's the attorney for the estate—but he isn't returning my calls."

"I haven't met Pohoke yet, so I can't tell you if that's intentional or if he's got bad office management skills." I followed Matt down the alley to the parking lot where presumably he'd left his battered pick-up truck. "The failure to return calls is generally the number one complaint that clients have about their attorneys. Of course, you're not a client, and he probably knows you're a journalist, so it's entirely possible he doesn't see any benefit in talking to the press about a client's estate."

"What else do you know about it? Have you seen the will?"

I shook my head. "I only heard about it from Gil a few minutes ago."

"And now you're going to appraise the quilts for the museum."

I didn't think Gil would mind Matt knowing I'd been retained, but the ethics rules relating to client confidentiality were too deeply ingrained for me to identify a client without her permission. "You'd have to ask her about that."

"I will," Matt said as we reached his truck. "And if she agrees, will you let me tag along when you go to view the quilts? I'd never thought much about what happens to an artist's work after she dies. I'm starting to look into it, and Miriam's estate could provide some interesting real-life examples. The story might even get some attention from bigger publications than the *Cove Chronicles*. I've been trying to get some more exposure on the national scene."

During his previous career, he'd already had more exposure than anyone but a Hollywood A-list celebrity. That wasn't really what he wanted. He wanted respect, something to counter the impression that many people had, assuming he was nothing more than a pretty face. I'd been guilty of that initially, so I tried to make up for it by never acknowledging just how physically attractive I found him.

"You're getting ahead of yourself," I said. "You still need to get Gil's permission before I can share any information with you."

"Sometimes reporters—everyone really, even lawyers, I bet—have to take some chances and not worry too much about the consequences." With a look that told me he wasn't just talking about the story he wanted to write about Miriam's estate, he added, "Both professionally and personally."

CHAPTER FOUR

———

Matt gave me a ride home, where I immediately settled down to draft a proposed contract for my work on Miriam's estate and send it to Gil. Then I stayed up late to work on the report on the Bergman sisters' collection, finishing it the next morning, considerably ahead of schedule.

In the end, it had been an easy decision. I'd recommended acquiring three quilts that had historical value, including a lovely Tumbling Blocks quilt made by the sisters' great grandmother around the turn of the twentieth century. She'd been a friend of Maria Dolores, the first lighthouse keeper of Danger Cove. The museum had Maria's diary in its archives, and I had found a reference to her helping the Bergman sisters' ancestor with layering the Tumbling Blocks quilt top with its batting and backing. Between the beauty of the quilt and the connection to town history, it would be an excellent addition to the museum's collection. It was too fragile for permanent display, but it could be rotated in and out of the room that was dedicated to the lighthouse's history.

After emailing the report on the Bergman sisters' quilts to Gil, I checked my inbox, where the signed copy of the contract for inventorying Miriam's collection was already waiting for me. I felt the same sort of anticipation that I used to experience when a client came in with a new and challenging legal case to work on.

I printed out the contract for my records and was about to call the estate's attorney to arrange for access to the property when the doorbell rang. More often than not, it just meant one of the bank's prior customers didn't realize the branch had been closed and hadn't noticed the prominent sign I'd posted, redirecting them to the new location. Still, I went out to what used to be the ATM lobby and now served as a space for meeting with my clients and appraising their quilts.

A young man—either late teens or early twenties—in khaki pants and an ill-fitting navy blazer stood outside. His blond good looks and muscular build reminded me of the local prosecutor, Frank Wolfe, or at least what I imagined he'd looked like about ten years ago when he'd been the quarterback on the local high school team. No, I thought; this kid didn't play football, at least not in the quarterback position. He was already more solid than Wolfe, despite not having reached his full potential. Wrestling team perhaps.

Whatever his sport of choice, he was probably selling something to raise funds for his team. I wasn't heartless, but living in the very center of town in what was often mistaken for a commercial building meant that even more Girl Scout Cookie sellers and other similar fundraisers came to my door than people who were trying to visit their safe deposit box. I pointed at the *No Soliciting* sign beneath the one that advised customers that their bank had moved.

He held up a Tyvek envelope addressed to me. The upper left corner was printed with *Aaron Pohoke, Esquire*, in a fancy cursive font like lawyers in the days of Charles Dickens' *Bleak House* might have used.

I unlocked the door and let the young man into the converted ATM lobby.

"Are you Keely Fairchild?"

I nodded.

"I'm Craig Pitts, and I work for Attorney Pohoke." He handed over the envelope. "He said to give this to you. It's a copy of a will and keys to the dead lady's house."

"You mean Miriam Stafford's?"

"Whatever." Craig was looking around the unadorned lobby with its long, narrow table and three wood chairs. "I heard you were a big shot lawyer in the city. Won a bunch of multi-million-dollar tort cases. That's what I want to do too."

"I don't know about big shot, but I was good at my job." I tugged on the too-well-sealed flap of the envelope. "And I was lucky enough to attract some clients with the potential for high awards."

"So why'd you quit?" Craig took the envelope back from me and opened it with as little obvious effort as if it hadn't been sealed at all before returning it to me. "And why move to Danger Cove of all places? I mean, it's not like there's much chance of getting a big case here. My boss does all right for himself, but he's been here forever, so everyone knows him, and there isn't much competition. But he only does maybe two or three personal injury trials a year, and none of them is all that big a deal."

"They're big deals to the clients." Keeping that fact front and center had likely had at lot to do with my past success, but had also added to the emotional burdens from my work. "Practicing law can be extremely stressful. It was time for me to find a little peace and quiet."

He snorted. "Yeah, Danger Cove's got that all right. Don't you ever miss the excitement?"

"Not really," I said, somewhat surprised at the thought. Retiring from the practice of law might not have been my choice, and there were moments when I wished I could help when someone needed the type of legal assistance I was good at, but overall I was content with my new career.

"Well, if you ever change your mind and go back to Seattle," Craig said, "I'd love to work with you. I'll be going to college there next year, so maybe I could do some sort of internship."

"I'll keep that in mind," I said, "but it's not likely to happen."

"I could show you how useful I can be by going to the dead lady's house with you, if you want," he said. "Aaron told me he didn't need me for anything else today if you wanted some help or just someone else to be there with you. I mean, it's got to be a little creepy to be in a strange house where the owner died recently."

"I appreciate the offer, but that won't be necessary. I won't be doing any heavy lifting, and I don't believe in ghosts."

"It still might be unsafe to be there alone. I mean, what if the killer comes back?"

It struck me then that I didn't know exactly how Miriam had died. Not that it really mattered. I wasn't afraid to be there alone, but I was curious. If Gil okayed Matt's joining me at Miriam's house, he might know more details about the murder. As he kept reminding me, he was a reporter after all.

"Despite what happened to Miriam," I said, "it's usually a nice, safe little neighborhood. I'll be fine on my own."

After a pause that suggested Craig was going to consider pleading his case some more, he said, "Okay," proving he had better instincts than some attorneys I'd seen in court who hadn't known when it was best to retreat and regroup. He dug in the chest pocket of his blazer for a sadly dog-eared stack of business cards with Aaron Pohoke's name and contact information printed in the same archaic script used on the envelope. Craig handed me one that had his own name and a cell phone number handwritten on the back. "If you change your mind, you can call or text me. Any time at all."

"Aren't you in school?"

He shook his head. "I graduated a semester early, and instead of starting college in January, I decided to wait until fall so I can earn some money for my school expenses. I didn't realize until too late that wrestling wasn't the best sport for getting a decent scholarship. I've got some savings from landscaping jobs in the summers, but nowhere near enough for an undergraduate degree, let alone both that and a law degree. The demand for outdoor work has been delayed by the late spring, so for now I'm just working part-time for Mr. Pohoke."

That kind of work ethic would help him in his legal career, assuming he didn't get disillusioned by the realities of a legal career in the course of his current job. "I'll keep you in mind if I do need any help with Miriam's estate. I don't really expect to though, and you'd probably be bored to death. Appraisal work is nowhere near as interesting and exciting to an outsider as legal work is."

That was why I'd chosen the new career, after all. Some of the repetitive work at Miriam's was going to be monotonous even for me, but at least there wasn't much risk that I'd pass out.

* * *

Craig Pitts left, and I dead-bolted the outer door before returning to the inner sanctum of my home. What had once been the main lobby and teller space was now my living room and kitchen.

I emptied the contents of the envelope onto the peninsula that divided the two areas and also served as the dining table. Inside was, indeed, a copy of Miriam Stafford's will and a pair of shiny new keys. There was a sticky note attached to the will: "Read this. Your client's interest extends to the entire contents of house. Changed locks this a.m. Entrusting the keys to you as an officer of the court." The signature was illegible—lawyers had somehow escaped their well-deserved reputation for bad handwriting, possibly because there were so many other reasons to tell jokes about us—although the name did seem to start with a capital A and there was a tall squiggle in the middle that could have been a capital P.

I sat on one of the peninsula's stools to read the will. Most of the text consisted of the necessary but unremarkable boilerplate language. The only exception was one brief paragraph that set out the exact distribution of Miriam's assets. She'd given "the entire contents of the house" to the Danger Cove Historical Museum, with the remainder of the estate to her cousin, Herb Stafford.

I was pleased to see that there were no conditions on the bequest to the museum that would prevent the quilts from being sold. The museum didn't really have the resources to care for a hundred-plus quilts that had no historical value and not enough aesthetic value to justify the cost of storing them. As long as the quilts didn't have to be retained by the museum, they could be bought by people who would use and appreciate them, and the proceeds could be added to the museum's general fund.

With the report on the Bergman sisters' quilts done ahead of the deadline, my schedule was clear for the next few days. Except of course for the impossible task of saving the quilt guild from eviction, but I couldn't do anything about that until my appointment with Jack Condor later today.

I considered doing some work in the vault in preparation for showing it to Matt. I could perhaps move some of the more revealing contents into storage until after he'd seen the space, and then I wouldn't have to worry as much about his reaction. I even started reviewing what I felt comfortable with him seeing and what I didn't, but I kept getting distracted by thoughts of Miriam's quilt collection.

It didn't take long before I gave in to the siren call of more than a hundred quilts waiting for me to study them. Preparing for Matt's visit to the vault could wait a little longer.

I sent Gil Torres a text, letting her know that I'd be working on the inventory until about 3:00 today, and that Matt had asked if he could observe. I didn't get an immediate response, so I packed my quilted messenger bag and headed out solo.

Half an hour later, I was heading up the driveway of Miriam's house, the strap of my bag digging into my shoulder with the combined weight of a digital camera that took better pictures than my phone, a laptop, and Barbara Brackman's hardcover reference book, *Encyclopedia of Pieced Quilt Patterns*.

Out of the corner of my eye, I caught a glimpse of a woman trotting out from the back door of the house to my right, the one with the *For Sale* sign in the front yard. She was tiny, barely five feet tall, and small-boned with a sharp, elfin face. She wore an ankle-length muumuu large enough to cover three people her size. It was made out of a lovely purple batik that would have been a nearly irresistible temptation to any quilter with scissors in her hands. As if prepared for such an attack, the woman was carrying a box large enough to serve as a shield against anyone trying to snip patches from her dress.

She stopped at the barrier of the white picket fence that separated the two properties.

"Excuse me." Her voice was high-pitched and squeaky. "Are you from the lawyer's office?"

"Sort of." I went over to see what she wanted. Up close, I could tell she was older than I'd thought originally, probably in her mid-fifties instead of mid-thirties. "I'm Keely Fairchild. I've been hired to inventory Ms. Stafford's quilts."

"Oh, good." She shoved the box in my direction, and I caught it automatically. It was heavier than it looked. Or perhaps it only seemed that way, since I was already burdened with everything in my messenger bag.

She explained, "This came for Miriam a few days ago. The mail carrier knows not to leave any packages out on the front porch, but the other delivery services don't know she died. I was afraid some creep would steal it, so I've been holding it for her. For her heirs, I mean."

"I can take it inside the house."

"What should I do if more packages are delivered?"

"That's a bit outside my job description," I said. "I'll ask the attorney to get in touch with you, though."

"Good. I'm Dani Hudson, and the landline is listed under my husband's name, Lou Hudson. The attorney can call me any time. I'm usually at home."

"I'll let him know." I nodded at the *For Sale* sign. "It must be a lot of work, keeping a place ready to sell."

Dani glanced over her shoulder as if she'd forgotten the sign was there. "I've gotten used to it. We've had it on the market for a while."

"If the inside is as nice as the outside, I'm sure you'll get more interest now that spring weather is finally here." My arms were starting to ache. I couldn't imagine how someone as petite as Dani had been able to carry the box across the yard with what had seemed to be remarkable ease. "I'd better get to work now. Thanks for watching out for Ms. Stafford's package."

"One more question if you don't mind," Dani said. "Can you tell me what's going to happen to Miriam's estate? It's just that we were neighbors for something like thirty years, and it's probably been ten years since anyone on this street has sold a house. Some folks were already worried that whoever buys our house could change the character of the neighborhood, and now there will be someone new in Miriam's house too. What if her estate sells to someone like Jack Condor? They might tear it down and put up something terrible. That's what Condor does, I've heard."

"I really don't know what the estate's plans are," I said. "You should talk to Aaron Pohoke about it."

"Oh, I know him," Dani said, her face brightening. "He represented my father's estate years ago. You don't have to ask him to call me. I've still got his number, so I'll call him."

I hoped Aaron would be better at returning her call than he'd been with Matt's. And I really hoped I could make it to Miriam's front steps before my arms gave out and I dropped the box. "I'll let him know to expect your call."

"One more thing." Dani leaned over the fence, the excess swathes of purple batik catching on the pointed pickets. "Do the police know what happened to her? Or who did it? With my husband away on business, I've been a little nervous at night. I never used to feel that way, but it's different now. Plus, it makes it hard to convince prospective buyers of our house that it's a nice neighborhood. They might believe me more if I could assure them the killer was caught and the motive was something that had nothing to do with this street being dangerous."

"I just appraise quilts. I don't know anything about the investigation," I said. "You probably know more about what happened to Miriam than I do."

"The police thought so too, and they were very nice, but I could tell they were disappointed that I couldn't tell them anything useful. We do watch out for each other on this street, keeping an eye out for strangers and that sort of thing." She nodded at the increasingly heavy box in my arms. "Like making sure packages are safe. But I didn't see anything unusual in the days before her body was found. She must have been killed at night, when I was asleep. Or perhaps when I was out running errands. My husband didn't see anything either. He was away on a business trip. He hasn't been home since then, in fact. I haven't told him about Miriam yet. He's going to be really upset."

"He was close to Miriam?"

"Not particularly. She didn't spend much time with people. We invited her to the neighborhood events, like the July 4th barbeque, and to our holiday open houses, but she was never interested. She preferred to be in her sewing room, making her quilts." Dani wrapped her arms around her ribs, making it even more obvious that the muumuu was several orders of magnitude too big for her frame. "It's just that my husband really wants to sell the house and move to a bigger city. I don't really want to leave Danger Cove, but living so far from an international airport is a burden for him, considering all the travel he does."

It was becoming obvious that Dani was lonely and wanted a friend she could gossip the day away with. In other circumstances, I wouldn't mind chatting a little longer, but not today. Besides the fact that my arms were threatening to give out from the weight of the package, I was feeling a little anxious about my appointment later today with Jack Condor. I needed to soak up as much of the soothing energy of Miriam's quilt collection as possible before then so I didn't pass out in the middle of negotiating with the guild's landlord.

CHAPTER FIVE

———

I finally managed to excuse myself without being too rude to Dani. Inside Miriam's little rust-colored house, the air was stale and stuffy from being unoccupied for so long. I set the package on the floor just inside the front door. Then I opened a few windows and shrugged out of my too-warm jacket and—I couldn't help myself—did a little snooping in the parts of the house I hadn't seen the last time I was here. Perhaps I could find some business records, possibly even a detailed inventory of the quilts.

The table in the eat-in kitchen had apparently served as Miriam's desk. It looked like there had been a computer tower there, probably confiscated by the police, so now only the monitor, printer, and a tangle of cables and cords remained. Above the table was a huge bulletin board with a calendar and assorted appointment cards and receipts affixed to it with sewing pins. But no inventory and no drawer or filing cabinet that might have contained anything related to the sale of Miriam's quilts.

I was going to check the bedroom next, but as I reached for the doorknob, I felt a chill, like the proverbial ghost walking over my grave. Despite what I'd told Craig Pitts about not being afraid of ghosts, something seemed to be warning me away from that room. Before my syncope diagnosis, I hadn't paid much attention to the signals my body sent me, but since then, I'd learned that ignoring those signals would more often than not end with me unconscious.

I had to check the bedroom eventually since it was likely at least one quilt was on the bed in there, but it didn't have to be done right this minute.

I returned to the front of the house to settle down to work. Before I touched any of the quilts, I retrieved a pair of white cotton gloves from my bag to protect the textiles from the naturally-occurring oils on my hands. Then I collected all of the quilts in the room and tossed them into a single pile next to the quilting frame. Like the quilts in the sewing room, these all had neat little tags on them, noting the name of the design, plus something that looked like an inventory number and a price. If I were lucky, that information matched records on the missing computer.

Three weeks had passed since the death, so the computer might have been returned to the estate's attorney by now. I'd have to ask him if I could look at Miriam's electronic files, but I couldn't wait until I had them before starting the inventory. There wasn't much time before the next museum board meeting, and Gil was counting on having the information on Miriam's quilts by then. If I worked through the weekend, I could get this project done before I had to drop it and work on other projects that would be due soon.

I started a spreadsheet on my laptop, creating columns to jot down the basics: the information on the tag, a note about the color scheme, and what size bed it would be appropriate for. After I finished keying in the data about each quilt, I piled it on the leather recliner against the wall.

By the third quilt, it had become obvious that there was something odd about the pricing: it was far too low to turn a profit. If there'd been just one like that, it could have meant that the specific quilt hadn't attracted any buyers at a more profitable price and had been marked down for clearance. But three of them in a row? And with the tags pristine, showing no indication that there had been a higher price once? That didn't seem likely.

I went into the back of the house and pulled five quilts at random from the hidden storage space. It didn't take long to confirm that every single one had a tag with a price too low for its maker to earn a living wage.

I hadn't known much about the cost of quilt supplies before I moved to Danger Cove. Since then, I'd observed quilters' excitement over certain fabric designers and manufacturers along with their sometimes sheepish admissions that they'd spent far more than they'd intended on some of the more expensive brands. I'd recognized some of those pricey designer fabrics in Miriam's workroom, and even if she'd used them sparingly by mixing them in with less expensive materials, the prices on the labels were only about a hundred dollars—sometimes even less—above what I estimated the quilts had cost to make. Add in some transaction costs, and Miriam couldn't have done much better than break even on the sale of her quilts.

It wasn't uncommon for hobbyists to sell off some or all of their quilts at cost, because they enjoyed the process of making them more than they appreciated owning the finished product. If they recouped enough money from the sale to buy the materials for their next project, they were happy. But Miriam had purportedly been a businesswoman without any other visible means of support.

Something was definitely wrong here. I'd have to let both the museum and the estate's attorney know, but first I needed more evidence to back up my suspicions.

I returned to the living room, and I'd finished looking at the next five or six quilts—all similarly undervalued—when the front doorknob rattled, and then someone knocked.

I'd have ignored it if not for the possibility it was Matt. Gil might have told him I'd be here, and I wouldn't mind some company. The place wasn't as creepy as young Craig Pitts had suggested, but the lighting everywhere except directly above the quilting frame was dreary, and the overall floor plan was more cramped and claustrophobic than I was used to.

I opened the door to find Herb Stafford standing there, taking the last few puffs from a cigarette. He seemed to be wearing the same clothes as yesterday, or else an identical unbuttoned flannel shirt over a stained white T-shirt and faded jeans.

"What are *you* doing here?" he asked. "I didn't hire you, and I'm not paying you."

"The estate's attorney has authorized me to do an inventory of the quilts."

"I heard that someone claimed to have found a will, and I'm not supposed to be in charge of my own inheritance." He shrugged. His voice was surprisingly calm. Perhaps my revelation yesterday that the quilts weren't as valuable as he initially believed had softened the blow of learning he'd been at least partially disinherited.

"So you've talked to Aaron Pohoke and seen the will?"

"Not yet," he said. "I got a message at the Ocean View B&B and set up an appointment to go talk to him later today. I need to be sure he didn't take advantage of my cousin when he wrote her will. Miriam wasn't in the best of health, you know, and she'd never had any social skills. Not like me. She couldn't read people, so she frequently thought people were looking out for her best interest when they weren't. Sometimes the other way around, too. She sometimes thought I was trying to scam her when I was really trying to protect her, and then I had to listen to her holier-than-thou lectures on personal responsibility."

It was hard for me to associate good people skills with Herb Stafford, but I couldn't discount his concerns entirely. I'd heard too many stories about unscrupulous estate-planning attorneys who'd abused their clients' trust. I had to hope Miriam's lawyer wasn't one of the bad apples. Not just for Miriam's sake, but also for Gil Torres's sake. It wouldn't reflect well on the museum if there were even so much as a rumor that the bequest had been the result of undue influence.

"I don't know Mr. Pohoke personally or professionally," I said, "but I understand he's been a fixture in the Danger Cove legal community since time immemorial. No one—especially not a lawyer—stays in business that long if they're shady."

"I hope you're right." Herb knelt to stub out his cigarette next to the existing black smears on the cement porch. "It's just that it's weird that Miriam didn't at least provide for me to get the family pictures. I had a fire in my apartment a few years ago and lost all of mine."

Now that he mentioned it, the wording of the will was a bit odd. Even though I wasn't an estate planning expert, I'd written my fair share of wills. Many of my personal injury clients hadn't had much in the way of assets when they first came to me, but once they'd received their compensation, they'd realized they needed an estate plan, and I was the only attorney they knew. Out of the hundreds of wills I'd worked on, I couldn't remember a single instance where anyone had provided for the contents of their house to go to someone outside the family.

Giving the contents of the house to close family members made far more sense than giving it to someone who had no personal attachment to it. Pictures and knickknacks were generally of purely sentimental value, things that only family members might care about. Some of the other items, like clothes, furniture, and the contents of the kitchen had some slight value on the secondary market, but in my experience, the heirs usually trashed most of that stuff, sometimes having to pay to get it taken away, rather than profiting from it.

And yet Miriam's will had clearly stated that everything inside the house was to go to the museum, not to her cousin.

Fortunately, it wasn't my problem, and I couldn't afford to waste time worrying about it right now. "You'll have to take that up with Mr. Pohoke."

Herb peered past me, into the living room. "It's just that I'd really hate for anything to happen to the family pictures before the estate gets resolved. Would you mind if I at least made sure they're secured? Once I know they're safe, I'll ask the museum not to throw them out. I'd even be willing to buy them from the museum."

"I don't have the authority to let you in." My stomach churned, threatening to escalate from slight discomfort to full-on nausea. "The best I can do is to let the museum know that you'd be interested in any pictures."

"I could help with your work while I'm here," he said. "It's not like I've got anything else to do around here, and I can't leave town until I work things out with the estate's lawyer."

I didn't have the time or patience to argue with Herb. I'd been hoping that before the end of today I'd have a solid grasp of the scope of the work here and I'd have seen at least one quilt that the museum might want to keep and add to its collection of locally made quilts. So far, all I had was an upset stomach and an uneasy feeling that something was fishy about Miriam's quilt business.

Perhaps I should have brought the young wrestler-turned-lawyer-wannabe from Aaron Pohoke's office after all. I didn't really think Herb would get violent right here on the front porch, in plain view of the entire neighborhood, but a witness inside the house with me would make it even less likely that matters would get out of hand.

CHAPTER SIX

———

"You need to leave now." I gripped the door, partly so I could close it before Herb could block me, and partly to make sure that if the confrontation made me lightheaded, I'd have something to lean on. "You can take it up with the estate's attorney when you see him."

I thought Herb was going to argue, but we were both distracted by the sound of jaunty whistling coming toward us. I didn't recognize the tune, but it was definitely a happy one. Even as irritated as I was with Herb, the whistling made me want to smile, and my stomach settled down.

I looked past Herb to see a mail carrier I'd never met before coming up the driveway. He was average height, probably in his early forties. His deeply tanned face didn't have any obvious wrinkles, and he was in excellent physical condition, as evidenced by the muscular calves revealed by the shorts of his uniform, but he had a receding hairline that left most of the top of his head bare. His super-sized mailbag made my quilted messenger bag—which held more than I could comfortably carry for any great distance—look like a child's accessory.

"Hello, new neighbors." The mail carrier's voice held a hint of an Hispanic background, more a matter of inflection or rhythm than an actual accent. "I'm Tony Flores, and I'm here to remind you that our first priority in the U.S. Postal Service is, was, and always will be you."

Herb glared at the mail carrier. "We were having a conversation here before you interrupted."

Tony didn't slow either his approach or his smile. "Sorry, man. Just trying to be helpful. You never know when someone might need a stamp or an envelope."

Even Herb couldn't resist the cheerful enthusiasm beaming in our direction. "Yeah, well, I suppose I should be leaving anyway."

The mail carrier held out his hand for a shake, but Herb was busy pulling out a cigarette. He brushed past without acknowledging the greeting.

Undaunted, Tony turned to me. "If there's anything you need"—he paused to wink at me—"anything in the way of stamps and mailing supplies, that is, all you have to do is ask. I'm here five days a week, Monday through Friday. Have been for close to ten years now. The substitute for this route is good too, but she's still new."

I felt a moment's disappointment that I didn't have Tony for my mail carrier. I loved my renovated bank building, but I couldn't recall ever saying more than "hello" to my own mail carrier. In fact, I couldn't even say whether it was the same person all the time or a new one every day. "I'm not actually moving in here. I'm just doing some work for the estate."

"My heart is broken." He placed his hand over the left side of his chest and sighed dramatically. "I can't bear losing you to another mail carrier."

"You could always request a transfer."

"No, no," the mail carrier said with exaggerated sorrow. "That would break the hearts of all my beloveds on this street. I couldn't do that to them."

"You're a good man, Mr. Flores, putting their wellbeing ahead of yours."

He took an exaggerated stagger backwards. "You wound me again with all this mister stuff. Call me Tony."

"Of course. And I'm Keely Fairchild."

"I've heard of you," he said, turning serious. "A quilt appraiser, right? Miriam always wanted to get your opinion of the antique she has on her wall. She showed it to me once and asked me what I thought of it. All I could tell was that it was orange, and it looked old, but what do I know about quilts, huh?"

"I've seen it, and it is lovely. I'll be doing a more thorough appraisal for the estate, but I'm confident it will turn out to be an antique."

"She'd have liked that," Tony said. "It's just sad she never got to give you its history. I can't remember much of what she said about it. I think it was made by some relative of hers, and somehow it got damaged, but she rescued it. She had trouble finding the right fabrics to replace some damaged pieces. Eventually she found what she needed at an estate sale near Seattle. I remember thinking it must have been traumatic for her to go that far to find the fabric. She hardly ever left the house—I could see her through the picture window, working at the quilting machine, almost every day when I delivered her mail—although she did get out to do her errands locally. Mostly, she was just terrified to go beyond the borders of Danger Cove. And yet, she went practically all the way to Seattle for what she needed to fix that quilt. Which, to tell the truth, I thought was kinda ugly, but, hey, to each her own."

"Cheddar quilts are something of an acquired taste for many people," I said, "but I'm sure we'll find someone to cherish it."

"Cheddar, huh?" Tony grinned. "Now you're making me hungry. I don't suppose you're free to have lunch with me? I just need to finish this street before I take a break."

"I'm afraid not," I said, genuinely regretful. "I'm already running behind schedule."

"Maybe another time." Tony's face grew solemn again. "You will make sure that Miriam's quilts are treated with respect, won't you? She lived for them. Probably died for them too."

"You think she was killed because of her quilts?"

"I don't know," he said. "I was the one who first realized something was wrong, you know. She wasn't at her quilting machine when I came by for three days in a row. Sometimes our schedules didn't align perfectly, so the first day, I thought she'd stepped into another room and I'd just missed her. The second day, I thought it was a little odd, but she might have had an appointment or something. But when it happened again on the third day, I knew something was wrong. Called 9-1-1 and wouldn't leave until the police went inside and found her body. I got a reprimand for taking too long on my route that day, but I didn't care. I had to know what had happened. No one else cared, and everyone deserves to have someone who will notice if they're dead or alive."

"I was right before," I said. "You are a good man. Miriam was lucky to have you as a friend."

"I see too many lonely people in this job," Tony said. "Used to be, folks would at least send letters and cards to family and friends who lived alone. Nowadays, no one does that anymore. It's sad."

"Being alone might not have bothered Miriam. I heard she wasn't much of a people person."

"That's just because hardly anyone ever made the effort to get to know her." He glanced over his shoulder in the direction Herb had scurried off. "Like her cousin. He came around maybe once a year. He never sent her any letters either. Of course, she never sent him any either. Her mail was mostly packages for her quilt business. At least one a week, which is how I got to know her. She'd come to the door if she saw me with something more than envelopes. It was like my visits were the highlight of her week. Or at least the packages were, but I did try to spend a few minutes with her, and she seemed to appreciate the attention."

The murder was none of my business, but I couldn't help asking, "Did Miriam have any friends at all besides you? I know that Herb's her only blood relative, but what about other people who might have cared about her? Members of the quilt guild maybe?"

"There was this one guy who'd been hanging around lately. I introduced myself once. He said his name was Wayne Good. She acted like he was her boyfriend, but he's probably ten years younger than she was. I know I shouldn't judge, and it wasn't just his age that made them seem like an odd couple. It was more that Miriam wasn't much of a socializer, and he seemed like the kind who really liked to party. I know she liked him, though, and she'd even stop quilting when he came to visit. Maybe he was an acquired taste, like that orange quilt on her wall, but I have to say, I wouldn't turn my back on him if he was anywhere near my mail pouch."

A battered pick-up truck came up the street and pulled into Miriam's driveway.

Tony watched over his shoulder as the truck came to a stop and the engine was turned off. "I see you've got company, and I've got appointed rounds to complete. Just remember, we deliver for you."

*　*　*

Matt Viera climbed out of the pickup and sauntered over to Miriam's front porch. "Has anyone ever told you that your lawyer face is both scary and pretty?"

"No one who lived to tell the tale," I said.

"I guess I'm special, then." He held up a hand to stop me from disagreeing with his self-assessment. "Before you have me arrested for trespassing, I'm allowed to be here. I talked to Gil, and she said it's okay for me to observe your work. You should have a text from her by now."

"I must have missed the ping." I realized belatedly that I shouldn't have left my phone inside the house, tucked into the pocket of the jacket I'd taken off when it had proven too warm to wear in the stuffy house. It wasn't so much that I might have needed backup for dealing with Herb, but I'd promised Dee's granddaughter that I'd never go too far away from my phone in case I felt a syncope episode coming on and needed to call for help.

Matt might not share all his secrets with me any more than I shared my own with him, but I knew him well enough to be convinced he wouldn't lie to me. If he said Gil had given her permission, then I was confident she had. "Come on in."

He raised his eyebrows. "You trust me that much?"

"Sure." I hadn't always trusted him—and I would still do the responsible, professional thing by checking my text messages to confirm what he'd said—but I'd come to believe that he wouldn't do anything underhanded just for a story. "It's not like I'm giving you the combination to my vault."

"A guy can dream."

Matt followed me into the living room where I collected my phone to confirm that Gil had authorized his visit. Her text did give me permission to discuss my work for the museum, just as Matt had claimed. Gil had also attached a press release that had been sent to the *Cove Chronicles* already, acknowledging that the museum had been named as the beneficiary of a quilt collection and I had been hired to inventory and appraise it.

While I was reading, Matt had been giving the entire room a quick once-over. That done, he headed over to the antique cheddar quilt on the wall. "That one's old, right?"

I put away my phone and went over to join him. "Yes, probably from the early 1800s. That was the peak of cheddar quilts' popularity."

He turned around to squint at the quilt on the machine dominating the space. "And that one?"

"A contemporary cheddar quilt."

"I'm guessing the antique is valuable, but what about the newer one?" Matt started patting down the plethora of pockets in his cargo pants, presumably searching for a pen and paper. He did have a smartphone, but he was a bit of a Luddite when it came to taking notes.

"That's a bit tricky." I debated whether to share with him my suspicions that there was something off about Miriam's business. I could really use someone to bounce my concerns off in case I was letting my professional paranoia get the better of me. Preferably someone familiar with the art world and who understood that pricing wasn't necessarily proportional to the amount of time spent creating a handmade item. Matt would definitely understand that. And I did trust him not to publish what I told him if he promised not to. "This has to be between you and me for now. Completely off the record."

"Sure." He stuck the pen and paper into separate pockets apparently chosen at random and then crossed his arms over his chest. "It must be something explosive if it's got you stumped."

"I don't know about that, but it's definitely puzzling." I led Matt over to the stack of quilts on the recliner and flipped the top one's tag so he could read it. "All of her quilts have these little tags with the block's name, an inventory number, and a dollar amount."

He peered at it. "Seems pretty straightforward to me. Not all artists are good at the business side of things, but a surprising number of them manage to keep records like that for their merchandise."

"It's not the existence of the tags that's bothering me, but what's on them." I pointed to the price: three hundred twenty-five dollars. "That can't be right. The supplies alone for a quilt that size, without including anything for the artist's time, would be at least three hundred dollars."

"That's the art world for you," Matt said with a shrug.

"The art world, yes, but from what I'm told, Miriam was doing this as a business, not just for the love of quilting. There wouldn't be any profit at that price."

"Maybe she didn't care about the money." He glanced around the sewing room. "It's not like she lived a luxurious lifestyle."

"She didn't scrimp either. Come look." I gestured for him to follow me into the kitchen, where I pointed at the wall above the table.

Matt leaned over the table to study the contents of the bulletin board. All around the quilt-themed calendar in the center were assorted bits of paper pinned in neat rows. Above the calendar, all by itself, was a yearlong pass to the Danger Cove Historical Museum. The right side had a collection of business cards lined up alphabetically. One was missing, but the remaining cards were for things like plumbers, electricians, car mechanics, or else places that delivered groceries or takeout food. The left side of the calendar was dedicated to receipts, including several from the Smugglers' Tavern and events associated with the Lighthouse Farmers' Market. Along the bottom of the calendar were three rows of appointment cards. Most of them were for a variety of doctors, but the entire bottom row was dedicated exclusively to The Clip and Sip. There were some old cards from the previous year, when she'd had appointments every two months or so, but for the eight weeks before her death, she'd started to go every single week.

I waited for Matt to lean back from his intense study of the various papers before I said, "I think Miriam's definition of 'luxury' had more to do with experiences, like going to the farmers' market and the museum, and less to do with things. Except for her quilt stash, of course."

"Okay, so she had a comfortable lifestyle," Matt said. "Maybe she had a source of income other than the quilts. She could have been living on disability. My source at the *Chronicles* said she was in poor health. Some kind of lung condition."

"I suppose that could explain it," I said. "It's just that her cousin said she didn't have any other source of income, and he definitely believed Miriam was making good money with her business. He was shocked when I told him how relatively little the entire collection was worth. Of course, he could simply have been wrong about his cousin's finances. The mail carrier told me Herb didn't visit here very often."

Matt dropped into one of the chairs facing the bulletin board. "Where did she sell her quilts? If she consigned them somewhere, they'd have records of the sales."

I pointed at the collection of receipts on the bulletin board. "It looks like she might have had an occasional booth at the Lighthouse Farmers' Market on holidays, but from what her cousin said, she did most of her business online, and I don't have those records."

"Maybe you're reading the tags wrong." Matt stood up and headed for the living room. "What if they're just for her use, and she'll remove them before she ships the quilt? The dollar amount could be the cost of supplies, rather than the retail price."

I followed him into the front of the house. "The answers are probably on her computer, but it looks like the police confiscated it."

He sorted through the tags on the quilts stacked on the recliner. "And you're not exactly eager to ask Detective Ohlsen if you can see what's on the hard drive, are you?"

"Ohlsen's okay." It was more the idea of having to deal with anyone else at the police station that made me reluctant to do it. Ohlsen listened to everyone respectfully, but that wasn't true of some of the other officers.

Matt gave up digging through the tags. "Why does any of it matter anyway? You can put the right price on them for the museum's use, so they'll get the full value."

"Two things," I said. "First, if I knew what Miriam sold her quilts for in the past, it would be extremely helpful for assigning a value to the ones she hadn't sold yet. The prices are going to depend in large part on what her reputation was within the cheddar quilt community."

He looked at me skeptically.

"There's a community for everything these days," I said, "now that aficionados can find each other online. If Miriam was something of a cheddar celebrity, she might have been able to charge more than what someone else could."

"Okay. Why else do you want to know what the tags mean?"

"If I'm right, and she was selling them for cost, it might mean that something shady was going on. I wouldn't want the museum to be associated with that."

"Shady how?"

"I don't know exactly. It's possible she was stealing her supplies. A while back, one of the clerks at Sunny Patches told me they'd been warned about a woman—not around here, but in the national news—who was selling quilts online for ridiculously low prices. Nobody could figure out how she could afford to do it until she was caught red-handed, unrolling a bolt of fabric and stuffing the material inside her clothes. It turned out she'd been stealing all her supplies from big fabric stores."

"You think Miriam might have been doing that?"

"Not really." I smoothed the top quilt in the stack on the recliner. "Sunny Patches is small enough that someone would have noticed if enough fabric for several quilts went missing, and I'd have heard about it. Besides, from what the mail carrier said, she got a lot of packages, so it sounds like she bought a lot of her supplies online. She might have been using a stolen credit card, I suppose."

"Not if she was shipping things to her own address," Matt said. "Too easy to get caught."

"Maybe I'm just imagining a problem. I tend to do that. It's part of my legal training. We're taught to anticipate the worst-case scenario, so we can take steps to minimize the risks or at least minimize the negative consequences if things do go wrong."

"Is that why you always expect the worst from me?"

I'd definitely done that when we first met, acting as if he were the lowest of muckrakers instead of a reputable journalist. I was still expecting the worst now, at least when it came to sharing any of my secrets, for fear that he would somehow abuse that trust.

"It's not personal," I said. "I expect the worst from everyone. But I do hope I'm wrong in this case, and Miriam was just an enthusiastic hobbyist who didn't care about the money as long as she brought in enough to keep quilting. She probably had some other source of income that her cousin didn't know about. The estate's attorney can probably tell me. If she was receiving disability, he might even have handled her case."

"What are you going to tell Gil?"

"Nothing until I'm sure that something's wrong. First I'll need to check to see if anyone who sells fabric locally has experienced the degree of shoplifting that would be necessary to account for all of Miriam's quilts."

"It could be tricky for you to do that while it's known that you're appraising Miriam's estate. People might well figure out that you suspect her of shoplifting." Matt pulled out his notebook and pencil again. "On the other hand, no one knows I've got anything to do with Miriam's estate. Why don't I ask around for you?"

"What's in it for you?"

"It might turn into a story on shoplifting in the arts," he said. "But what I'm really counting on is that it'll show you how much you need me."

CHAPTER SEVEN

———

Aaron Pohoke's office was in a storefront located right at a trolley stop on Main Street. Printed on the picture windows was a list of his "specialties," which seemed to include every single field of law that I'd ever heard of. He probably referred out the cases that a solo practitioner couldn't handle, like medical malpractice and product liability, the types of cases that my previous law firm was known for. Over the years, I'd worked with a number of small-town attorneys who'd referred cases to me, but never any from Danger Cove.

When I'd called for an appointment, Aaron's receptionist had encouraged me to come straight on over to his office. Apparently he'd set today aside, mostly free of appointments, to catch up on paperwork after being tied up in court all of last week.

Matt gave me a ride before heading off to do his own research, so it only took a few minutes to get to the attorney's office. The receptionist offered me a warm smile and ushered me straight in to see her boss. He remained facing the side extension of his desk, peering at the monitor and keying in the occasional bit of information. I wasn't sure if he was intentionally being rude—playing some sort of dominance game—or was simply so completely wrapped up in his work that he didn't notice our arrival. If it was a game, I knew the rules, and ignoring his ignoring me was the next play.

I dropped my heavy messenger bag into one of the visitor chairs and sat in the other one to observe him.

It was somewhat surprising that Pohoke was willing to key things into a computer directly instead of delegating it to an employee. He'd obviously attended law school well before the widespread introduction of computerized research and word processing to the practice of law. The skin on his face was papery and gray, his hands were almost one big liver spot, and his white hair was so fine I could see the veins on his scalp.

It didn't take long before he muttered, "Done," and clicked the mouse, presumably saving whatever he'd been working on. He turned to face me. "So, you're Keely Fairchild. I've read about you in the *NWLawyer* magazine. Never thought you'd consider opening an office here in Danger Cove."

"My office is purely for quilt appraisals," I said. "I'm officially retired from practicing law."

If he'd had any eyebrows left, they would have raised. As it was, his skepticism just resulted in an extra row of wrinkles above both eyes. "You're way too young to retire. That's the trouble these days, you know. All the experienced lawyers are quitting, and there's no one left with any experience. Just those young kids straight out of law school, and they're a nuisance to deal with. They may know the letter of the law, but they don't understand its spirit."

"It does take a few years before they gain a more realistic view of the practice of law, doesn't it?"

Aaron seemed to relax. At least, the wrinkles on his forehead diminished slightly. "I can't imagine you're here to discuss the state of the legal profession. Especially seeing as how you're retired."

"I've got some questions about Miriam Stafford's estate. Do you know when the police will be releasing her computer files? It would make my work quicker and more accurate if I knew a little bit about her past quilt sales."

"I'll give the detective a call," Aaron said, making a note on a legal pad. "Anything else?"

"It's a little delicate," I said. "I was wondering if you knew anything about her finances. There are some preliminary indications that she wasn't much of a businesswoman. I was wondering if she was actually trying to make a profit with her quilt sales or if she had some other source of income. A pension or disability benefits perhaps?"

"Not that I'm aware of." Aaron shuffled through a stack of files on his desk until he found the one he was looking for. He didn't open it, but set it in front of him, rubbing the cover as if he could read the contents through his fingertips. "As far as I know, she was making a good living from the quilt sales. She came in once to ask about the legalities of a home business. Nice to see a client come to me before they're in trouble, for a change."

"I know what you mean." It was a lot easier to anticipate and prevent problems when clients consulted an attorney early, before the worst-case scenario had already happened. Of course, most clients didn't care about making things easier for their lawyers.

"But that was Miriam for you. Always prepared and a stickler for doing things right." The hand patting the file froze, and he peered at me irritably. "I hope you don't think she was doing anything illegal. I know a lot of online sellers allegedly don't report their profit on their tax returns. Not Miriam. She would have reported every dime of income. Every penny."

"It's actually the opposite problem," I said, feeling a bit foolish about my suspicions in light of Aaron's conviction that Miriam was so righteous. "It looks like she didn't have any real income. Not once her expenses were subtracted. Of course, I'd need to see her sales records to know for sure."

Aaron lifted the file to scribble on a legal paid underneath it. "I'll see if I can get copies of what's on Miriam's hard drive if the police can't actually return the computer to me. They were hoping to get some leads on anyone who might have wanted her dead."

"What about Herb Stafford? He stopped by the house while I was there. He seemed a bit irritated that he won't be inheriting as much as he'd expected to."

"I've never met the man," Aaron said. "Miriam didn't really tell me much about him either. Just that he was her only living family member. He's got an appointment with me this afternoon. I'll know more then."

Aaron hadn't been particularly welcoming, and he hadn't shared anything that violated his duties to the estate, but he had cooperated by talking to me with such little notice. I could return the favor by telling him what I knew. "Herb stopped by Miriam's house and mentioned the possibility that his cousin had suffered from 'undue influence' in the execution of her will, which makes me wonder if he's already been to see his own lawyer to ask about his rights. Herb was pretty anxious to get inside Miriam's house. He said he was mostly interested in securing some family pictures, but I couldn't tell if that was just an excuse. He might have wanted to look around the house some more so he could see if there was anything in there that's valuable enough to justify the expense of contesting the will. He was definitely angry when I wouldn't let him inside."

"Killing angry?"

"Not really." I'd been relieved by the arrival of the mail carrier, although not because I was afraid of Herb. I'd felt more at risk from my own nervous system than from Miriam's cousin. "On the other hand, we were on the front porch at the time, and any number of people could have been watching. He might have acted differently if we'd been inside where no one could see him."

Aaron's eyes narrowed. "Don't take any chances while you're at the house. I don't want your estate suing me if anything happens to you out there."

He was as bad as I was about imagining the worst-case scenario. "I'll be careful. And I always have my phone close at hand for emergencies." I pulled it out of my jacket pocket to demonstrate.

"Good, good." Aaron finally opened Miriam's file. He flipped to the back of the folder, revealing several yellow sheets torn from a legal pad and covered with illegible handwriting. "I'm not worried about a will contest. There isn't anything strange about the distribution, and I've got extensive notes from her appointments, listing her wishes in her own words."

"I did wonder about the wording a bit," I said. "It seemed odd that the personal effects would be distributed to a charity instead of to family."

"Normally, perhaps, but not so much in this case." He tapped the top page of notes. "I remember now. I asked her what she meant to give to the museum, and I even wrote down her answer here. She said there wasn't much in her house that anyone would care about, other than her quilts and 'the ability to experience life.' I asked her what she meant by that, and she told me to look it up. Apparently it's got something to do with Henry

David Thoreau. I'm afraid I never got the chance to do it. Perhaps her cousin will know what it means, but I doubt it had anything to do with family pictures. Miriam didn't strike me as a particularly sentimental person."

He was right about that much. There certainly hadn't been any family pictures on display in the main rooms. In fact, I hadn't seen any pictures of any sort, not counting the quilting calendar in the kitchen and some sketched-out designs on graph paper in the sewing room. Of course, I hadn't gone into the bedroom or poked inside any cabinets or drawers, so perhaps she had an album somewhere hidden away, and that was what Herb wanted.

"I also wondered why she didn't even mention the quilts in the will," I said. "I would have thought she'd be explicit about what she was giving the museum."

"I thought so too. But she said..." Aaron consulted his notes again. "Ah, yes, I knew I'd written it down. She said she wanted the museum to get every single thing inside the house. She wanted to be absolutely clear about it, and she was afraid that if she mentioned the quilts at all, they'd overshadow everything else."

That was odd, I thought. "There really isn't anything else in her house. Not even much in the way of furniture. Certainly nothing that the museum is likely to keep."

"You know as well as I do that it's impossible to really understand what a client is thinking. Miriam wasn't much of a people person, so it was even more difficult to get relevant information out of her than most clients. She would answer a simple 'how are you' with a bunch of statistics about her pulse, blood pressure, and pulmonary function tests." Aaron closed the file. "I did my job, and I've got the records to prove it, so I'm not worried about a threatened will contest. In all the years I've been in practice, I've never had a will successfully contested. It's not going to happen with this one either."

"You don't have to convince me," I said, gathering up my messenger bag to leave. "I'm just as glad, on behalf of the museum, that Miriam was vague about what she was bequeathing them. If she'd been more specific, she might have been tempted to put some restrictions on the bequest."

"Makes it easier for me too as the representative of the estate," Aaron said. "Monitoring what the museum did with the quilts would have been time-consuming, and I've got better things to fill my billable hours. Not that I won't do my job properly. And I would have written the restrictions into the will if she'd wanted them."

"Of course." I stood. "One last thing before I go. You said she'd consulted you on her business setup. Do you know what she called it? Perhaps I can find some records of her quilt sales online if I know that."

"That's easy," Aaron said. "She was doing business as Miriam's Cheddar Blocks."

* * *

The Danger Cove Historical Museum was across the street and to the right of Aaron Pohoke's office. I had enough time to stop in and see Gil if I wanted to, but I was reluctant to worry her with what might just be my worst-case-scenario habit running amok. I needed to do some more research before I shared my concerns, and that would take more time than I had before I caught a cab to go see the guild's landlord, Jack Condor.

While I considered joining the other locals enjoying the spring weather and admiring the view of the cove from the pier until it was time to leave for my appointment, I happened to see Officer Fred Fields coming out of the Cinnamon Sugar Bakery. Not exactly surprising, since it was his home away from home. Fred was in his mid-thirties and average in height, with an ever-increasing waistline despite the exercise he got from walking a beat.

Fred might be able to fill me in on some of the details of what had happened to Miriam. I headed in his direction, away from the pier, calling out a greeting as I crossed the street.

Fred guiltily tucked the distinctive pink and brown takeout bag into the pocket of his uniform jacket. His wife must have been on his case even more than usual about his diet, and he didn't want word getting back to her about his succumbing to temptation. As if someone like him, who took his job as a beat cop seriously by making his official presence as visible as possible, could do anything in a small town like Danger Cove without the news getting to his wife well before he got home.

"Where were you today?" he said when I reached the bakery. "I missed you at the stress support group meeting."

His anxieties manifested somewhat more benignly than mine did—with sugar cravings instead of unconsciousness—but we both belonged to a hospital-sponsored patient support group for dealing with stress. I did try to get to as many of the lunchtime meetings as I could, but the opportunity to view a huge collection of quilts was even better for reducing my stress levels than any other therapy. Usually, anyway. Not quite as much when the quilts were connected to a murder.

"I was at Miriam Stafford's house," I said. "I'm doing some work on her estate."

"Be careful," he said. "I mean, that cul-de-sac is a generally safe neighborhood, but there was an incident at her house a few weeks back, shortly before she died. Dispatch got a call about some kind of a scuffle there. It was all over by the time the officer arrived to check it out, and Miriam denied there'd been a problem, but it never felt right to me."

I wouldn't have been surprised if the caller had been Dani Hudson, but Fred would never share that information with me. He might bend the rules a bit, but he'd never breach confidentiality of an anonymous call.

"And then Miriam got killed about two weeks later. Really makes you wonder." Fred slid a hand inside the pocket where he'd tucked the pink and brown bag as if to reassure himself it was still there. "It's such a sad, sad case. The woman was smothered by her own quilts."

Fred didn't joke about crime, but I was so startled that I had to ask, "Seriously?"

"Seriously." He must have decided that it was futile to hide his bakery purchase, or else thinking about a murder in his town had pushed him over the edge, because he took out his pink and brown bag and pulled out a muffin with cinnamon streusel on top. "They found her sort of like an upside down version of the princess and the pea, with all the quilts on top of her instead of underneath her."

"Why didn't she just push them off?"

"That's what everyone wanted to know," Fred said. "She hadn't been drugged or knocked unconscious or anything. At first they thought maybe the quilts had been piled on top of her after she died, by whoever tossed the place. Like she might have died in her chair from a heart attack, and then the burglar had arrived afterwards and tossed the quilts on top of her so he wouldn't have to look at a dead body. But then they figured out she'd actually died from suffocation. They think the quilts were tossed on top of her while she lay back in the recliner, and then when she tried to push them off her, she couldn't. A healthy person wouldn't have had any trouble, but she had severely compromised lungs. Some genetic disorder. I don't remember what it's called, but it acts like severe emphysema. So when she struggled, the activity caused her to get breathless, which made it even harder for her to push the quilts off, and it just spiraled down from there."

"That's horrible." Not just the fact of the death, but also the unfairness of the situation. The very things that Miriam had loved so much, the things she'd spent so much of her life creating, had been used to kill her.

"Yeah." Fred grimly bit into the cupcake. After swallowing, he added. "What's worse is that Bud Ohlsen doesn't have any evidence that he hasn't gone over at least twenty times already without coming up with a solid suspect. Most likely the killing was just a random burglary gone wrong. Random crime is always the hardest to solve without any witnesses, and we haven't found anyone who saw anything useful. I'm especially worried because of how long it's been without any new information. It's way too early to declare this a cold case, at least publicly, but I think it's in the back of everyone's mind already. In a few more days, it'll have been a full month since the detectives exhausted their last lead. At that point, the case is probably going to be relegated to a quarterly review. Once that happens, it takes a miracle for an arrest to be made."

I knew how much that would bother Fred. If he could find the killer by willpower alone, he'd do it. Unfortunately, though, willpower wasn't enough, just as it was never enough to truly overcome stress or an addiction to sweets. The police needed something tangible. They needed viable suspects and admissible evidence.

"I'll tell Detective Ohlsen if I notice anything about Miriam's quilts that he should know about." It was too early to share my suspicions about Miriam's quilt business with the police in case I was wrong, but if I could confirm there had been something shady going on, it might be useful information for the investigation.

"That would be great." Fred perked up, either from my offer or from the effects of consuming the entire contents of the bakery bag. He crumpled the paper and tossed it into a nearby trash container. "Maybe Miriam was killed because of her quilts, so they were the cause of death in more ways than one. You'd know the right things to look for, in that case."

"I can't promise I'll notice anything useful," I said. "Her death by quilts could have just been a sad irony."

"Yeah." Fred glanced longingly over his shoulder at the door to the Cinnamon Sugar Bakery. "I hate irony."

CHAPTER EIGHT

The cab let me out in front of an ostentatious steel and glass structure located on the outskirts of Danger Cove in a sprawling group of similarly modern office buildings. From what I'd heard, they were all Jack Condor's doing. He'd tried to build similar monstrosities in the historic center of town, but at least those proposals had been blocked. Not that that ever stopped him from trying again with different sites.

I'd never met Condor formally, although he'd been pointed out to me at some museum event or another. As his receptionist let me into his office, I remembered that he usually wore a hat, presumably to cover the thinning of his hair. He dispensed with it in his office, which made him appear much less impressive, as if he'd magically shrunk six inches in height and lost half of the muscle mass of his still-beefy arms. I might have attributed his less impressive stature to his having sunk deep into the super plush carpeting of the office suite, but I thought it was more likely that I'd just never seen him at such close range before without dozens of other people circulating nearby to distract me from seeing him for who he really was. From just a few feet away, his sparkling white teeth gave him more of a creepy, Cheshire-cat smile than a Hollywood one.

"What can I do for you?" Condor said brusquely without bothering with any small talk on the way over to his minimalist wooden desk.

"It's about the quilt guild," I began as I settled into the solitary visitor's chair, but he cut me off with an impatient huff.

"Those old biddies? I can't wait until they're gone and I can finally get my money's worth out of that building."

Even a wide-eyed optimist—something I'd never been accused of being—would have been able to see that this conversation wasn't going anywhere good. It was pointless to ask for a long-term extension of the quilters' use of their meeting room, and such a request was likely to make him less reasonable, if that was even possible. A different tack was needed.

"Perhaps you have another property where they could meet," I suggested. "One that you're not ready to renovate just yet, that they could use until they find a more permanent location. The goodwill that comes from a gesture like that could be invaluable. Just about everyone in Danger Cove, including the town officials, is related to at least one of the guild members. That sort of personal connection can come in handy when getting approval for a development or finding tenants for the finished project."

"I don't need no senile old grannies endorsing my projects. I can get them approved and tenanted on my own." He threw himself into his chair with such energy I thought it would collapse. "Besides, they wouldn't even understand my plans. It takes someone who's young and hip to share my vision."

I tried to hide my skepticism. Condor wasn't exactly a hipster himself or any sort of visionary genius. Damping down my emotions like this wasn't good for me, and I could feel my blood pressure rising. Apparently I'd lost whatever patience I'd once had for dealing with fools in the two years since retiring from the practice of law. I was extremely tempted to tell Condor what I really thought: he was acting like a delusional idiot.

Instead, I settled for getting to my feet and saying, "There's nothing further for us to talk about then, so I won't waste any more of my time here. It would be better spent making sure the press knows about your part in the guild's precipitous relocation, as well as the benevolent action of whoever offers them a new space to use."

"Wait," Condor said, flashing his bright teeth at me in a misguided attempt at charm. "No need to have a hissy fit. If you had let me finish, I'd have told you about a way where we can all get something out of this situation."

"I'm listening." I remained standing and crossed my arms over my chest, aware that my body language would let him know how unimpressed I was, so he'd better come up with something good.

"I might be able to work something out with the quilters if you'd put in a good word for me with Miriam Stafford's probate attorney."

The museum's press release couldn't possibly have been published yet, but I didn't bother to ask how he knew I was involved with the estate. It was Danger Cove, after all, and the grapevine was faster than Twitter. Even if Condor, as the least-liked person in town, was the last to know something, that only meant it took an hour or two, rather than mere seconds, for him to hear the latest news. "Why would you do that?"

"I'm always looking for new projects," he said. "Miriam's property could be a real jackpot, and there's enough of a cloud on the title that I can snap it up for cheap. The house itself is worthless, of course, and the color is hideous, so anything that replaced it would be an improvement. The lot's big enough for a duplex. Barely, but I could make it work. No one spends much time in their yards these days anyway. Kids don't even play outside anymore. At least not at home. They can always go to Pacific Heights Park if they really want to be outdoors."

Pacific Heights Park was, indeed, a lovely place in the heart of Danger Cove. It offered marked spaces for soccer and lacrosse. For less structured activities, there were a few benches and picnic tables near the central fountain and the statue of Francis Drake. The local garden club even maintained a small rose garden there, filled with antique varieties that hadn't had the scent bred out of them.

Even so, a park couldn't replace a child's own yard for unstructured play. Plus, a duplex like what Condor was planning would be totally out of character for Miriam's neighborhood. Sticking a big house in the middle of all those tidy little ranches would be like using a modern polyester blend fabric to replace damaged cotton materials in a vintage quilt. The inappropriate insertion affected everything around it too, not just the one repaired block of a quilt or the one parcel of land in a neighborhood.

Besides, even if I shared Condor's vision for Miriam's house, I couldn't trade one client's best interest for another's. The temptation to tell Condor what he could do with his offer was overwhelming and giving in to it would definitely release some of the building stress. Unfortunately, I couldn't afford to alienate him completely. I might need to talk to him again to negotiate for a delay of a week or two on the eviction while arranging for a new location for the guild.

"I'm sorry," I said firmly and with as little hostility as I could manage, "but I'm not in a position to make any recommendations on the sale of the house."

He thought for a moment before saying, "You have a key to the place though, don't you? It would be worth something to me if I could spend an hour in there taking measurements and assessing the structural elements. I've already got the publicly available data, but there's nothing like a walk-through to really know a project and get a leg up on the competition."

"You know an awful lot about Miriam's house, considering it's not even on the market yet."

Condor's shrug was a bit too forced, as if he knew—or thought he knew—that he'd convinced me to work with him, and all he had to do was keep talking about his wondrous plans in order to seal the deal. "It's my job to know about available sites. Besides, in this case, I have a bit of a secret weapon. Miriam worked for another developer in town, Frank Dreiser. He wants to retire early, and we'd just concluded negotiations for me to buy his business when she died. He let it slip that he'd considered buying her house. Just goes to show you how bad a businessman he was. Shouldn't have told me anything before our deal was finalized."

"He couldn't have been too bad at his work if he can retire early."

This time Condor's shrug was real and irritated. "How would I know anything about his finances? All I know is how bad our deal is for him. He was in too much of a rush to unload the properties he was never able to develop, or he'd have gotten a better price from me. He'd be shocked if he ever found out how wrong he was about their value. He thought they were worthless, but that's because he doesn't have my vision. I just wish he wasn't leaving town right away, so he'd be able to see what he missed out on."

I wondered how long it had been since Dreiser had tried to buy Miriam's house. If it was recently, that gave him a motive for killing her, although it was a somewhat unlikely one. Still, it sounded like he was leaving town in something of a rush, possibly going far enough away that it would be difficult for the police to interview him if he ever became a suspect. "Where's he going?"

"Who cares?" Condor waved his hand airily. "I just know it's going to be soon. He insisted on spending all day here today, making sure he gets all the properties transferred, along with the files related to them, so I'll hand over the final installment on the purchase. He's been here since before I arrived this morning, going over the details with my assistant. I'll have to review everything myself later, of course, since Dreiser doesn't have my knack for seeing the potential in seemingly worthless property."

"He saw some potential in Miriam's property," I said. "It wouldn't have been easy to convince her to sell the house to him, the person who'd fired her. And yet, he apparently thought it was worth the effort to try."

Condor waved his hand dismissively. "Not my problem. All I know is that he'd been keeping an eye on the situation for years. Probably because he knew she was sick, so he could negotiate with her estate instead of with her. Even a bad businessperson can get something right once in a while. The property does have potential, but I'm going to be the one to cash in now that she's dead, not Dreiser."

And the public thought lawyers *were vultures*, I thought. Maybe they were to some degree, but as a group they'd long since been eclipsed by real estate moguls, Wall Street traders, and CEOs of prescription drug companies.

* * *

I made it clear to Jack Condor that I wasn't prepared to provide him with any inside information on Miriam's home, and he suddenly remembered he had a meeting with Edward

Kallakala, the town's mayor. Condor rushed off without bothering to walk me out of his office.

These days, I didn't rush anywhere, so I followed at my own, slower pace. From the reception area, I could hear voices in a nearby office. Condor's assistant and Frank Dreiser, most likely.

"You look like the boss just evicted your granny," the blonde receptionist said. A clear acrylic nameplate that identified her as Bonnie Lang hung from a three-tiered plastic inbox on her desk. "I see that expression a lot, but it's never as bad as you think. Everything works out for the best. At least, that's what the boss says."

"I'm not a big believer in things working out for the best," I said. "At least not without a whole lot of work on someone's part."

The blonde wrinkled her nose. "You're probably right. I bet you're the one who ends up doing all the work in your job too. Like me keeping this office running while the boss is off playing golf with his buddies."

My first impression of Bonnie hadn't led me to believe she was the brains behind the Condor empire. Her artificially large lips and heavy-handed makeup were as overdone as the bleaching of her hair. Now that I looked past the sparkly shadow and thick mascara, directly into Bonnie's eyes, I suspected that if things did, in fact, all work out for the best around here, it was most likely due to her efforts, not Condor's.

Perhaps I should have made my appointment with Bonnie instead of the boss. I doubted she could blatantly overrule Condor's decision about the quilt guild, but perhaps she'd be willing to help me in another way. I'd have really liked to meet Miriam's ex-boss and find out why he was in such a rush to leave town.

"I understand that Frank Dreiser is here. Any chance I could have a chat with him?"

"You want to do business with him instead of the boss?" Bonnie asked. "It's too late for that. Dreiser's retiring."

"I heard about the sale of the business," I said. "This is about something else. Someone else, actually. Miriam Stafford."

Bonnie frowned. "Sounds familiar, but I don't know her."

"She was murdered."

Bonnie leaned back in her chair. "If you think the boss did it, you're wrong. I know he's a greedy jerk and all, but he isn't violent."

"I never thought for a moment that he killed her," I said, with complete honesty. At least not intentionally. On the other hand, it was possible that he'd killed a few people with his greed and lack of empathy, making their lives so miserable that their immune systems weakened to the point where the first serious germ they encountered was enough to kill them. "Dreiser is a more likely suspect. He and Miriam had a history together, and not a good one."

"In that case, it must be time for my coffee break." Bonnie ducked down behind her desk to dig around in a bottom drawer. She popped up again with a faux designer handbag—I knew enough to know it was a knock-off, but not the name of the original—and got to her feet, teetering on stiletto heels as exaggerated as her lips and hair. She nodded toward the hallway that led in the opposite direction from Condor's private office. "While I'm gone, you absolutely, positively should not go near the first door on the right down there."

* * *

I knocked on the first door on the right and a moment later it flew open. Standing in the opening was a tall, glowering man in jeans that were faded to a blue that was almost white, and a denim shirt that was darker, but frayed along the edges of the cuffs. His face was as craggy as the cliffs overlooking the waters of Danger Cove, and his skin had that deeply wrinkled, leathery texture that comes from spending too much time working outdoors. I wasn't sure if he was a worn-out fifty-something or a comparatively young-looking sixty-something. More likely the latter, the right age for early retirement, assuming this was Frank Dreiser.

"I told Condor I'd get this done as soon as I could," the man snapped at me. "It's not my fault that he gave me someone incompetent to work with."

I looked past the presumptive Dreiser to a young man at the conference table. He appeared to be a contemporary of Craig Pitts, the teen who'd brought me the envelope from Aaron Pohoke's office. In every way but age, though, he was Craig's polar opposite. He was short and thin with the extremely pale skin—now blotchy from blushing at the criticism of his work—that redheads like him were famous for. He also seemed to be shy, rather than gregarious like Craig, and kept his eyes focused on the laptop in front of him. He continued to type without interruption.

"Condor didn't send me," I said. "I'm Keely Fairchild, and I'm doing some work for the estate of Miriam Stafford. Assuming you're Frank Dreiser, then it's my understanding that you knew her, that she used to be your employee. I was hoping you could spare me a minute to talk about her estate."

"I don't know anything about her life after she quit her job and left me hanging," he said, implicitly confirming his identity. "All I can tell you is that she was a lazy, lying thief. I once thought she might be different, but in the end she was just like every other woman I've ever known. Can't trust any of them." He tossed a glance over his shoulder at the teen who was pretending not to listen. "At least she was reasonably good at her job, unlike what you can hire these days."

I had to remind myself that I wasn't in a position any longer where I needed to jump to the defense of downtrodden women and underpaid workers, and it wasn't in my best interest to remind Dreiser that he was speaking to a woman who might find his sweeping insults offensive. Not while I needed to get more information out of him.

"You weren't completely over your irritation with Miriam." I didn't have any duty to keep Condor's statements confidential. He was a big boy, after all, and if he hadn't wanted his plans made public, he should have kept them to himself. "I understand you kept an eye on her house over the years since she left her job. Now Condor wants to buy it from the estate based on the information in your files."

A sly look came into Dreiser's eyes. "It's tempting to fight him for the property. There's a non-compete in the contract we signed, but by the time he could enforce it, I'd have flipped the house, made my score, and taken off for my retirement home in Mexico."

"That would take a while to do. I heard you were anxious to leave Danger Cove."

"I'm flexible," he said. "Given enough of an incentive, I could stick around for a little longer. I don't suppose you'd be able to let me inside Miriam's house to see exactly what condition it's in, would you? I'd make it worth your time."

If I told him the truth, that there was no way I'd let either him or Condor into the house, I'd never get any more answers out of him. Fortunately, I had a lot of experience at ducking questions. "Is the house that valuable? It seemed pretty ordinary to me. And I'm not convinced Condor will get the necessary permits to build the duplex he's got in mind. Not in that neighborhood."

Dreiser rolled his eyes. "Condor's an idiot. Always going for the impossible score, wasting time and money on projects that will never get approved. Better return on investment if you just take the small, fast wins and move on. That's what I did, and look where it got me: retiring to paradise by my sixtieth birthday. But not Condor. The stars in his eyes blind him to the real value of property. Like in this deal with me. All he got out of it was my mistakes, the property that isn't worth what it'll take to fix it up. I'd already written them off as a total loss, so the money Condor's paying me is a windfall. A particularly hefty windfall, given his unrealistic expectations."

The teen's typing had drifted to a stop. Condor couldn't be much easier to work for than Dreiser was, so my guess was that the young man was as entertained as I was by the two developers' diametrically opposed views of who had been the winner in the business deal. Dreiser should have had enough sense not to crow about his victory in front of his rival's employee. Of course, he could have been counting on the fact that if the teen did tell his boss about this conversation, it would bounce off Condor's massive ego.

"Is that what you'd do with Miriam's house if you bought it?" I asked. "Something small and fast?"

"Yeah." Dreiser turned to glare at the teen, who immediately resumed tapping away on his laptop. "Her house is going to go for cheap, because most buyers can't see past the cosmetic stuff, like that terrible exterior color. Miriam was always tidy, I'll give her that much, so I bet the inside is in pristine condition. Mostly all the place needs is a coat of paint on the exterior. Maybe inside too, if it's anything like the outside."

"So you've never been inside Miriam's house? Perhaps while discussing her decision to quit?"

Dreiser snorted. "You think I'd waste my time with a losing proposition like that? I told you, the key to success is to move on as fast as you can."

"Then why did you go to the trouble of investigating her house? I got the impression you had some pretty substantial notes in the files you handed over to Condor."

"Just doing what anyone in my business would do," Dreiser said. "At first, I considered suing her for leaving me in the lurch the way she did, quitting with no notice. Before I went to the trouble, though, I wanted to be sure she had sufficient assets to make it worth the effort. She didn't though. Nothing other than her house, so my attorney convinced me it would be best to just let her go. Especially since she wasn't in the best health, so all I had to do was watch the obits while I waited for her to die. Not a huge investment of time, compared to a lawsuit."

"She wasn't that old," I said. "Was her health really bad enough that she was likely to die young?"

"I'm no doctor," Dreiser said, "but she called in sick all the time, really made it hard for me to get any office work done. I only put up with it because if I fired her instead of waiting for her to quit, I'd have been sued for discrimination or something. And that would have been a real waste of my time."

"I won't waste any more of your time now." I'd been under the impression from Herb that Miriam had been fired, rather than quitting her job. I wondered if he'd gotten it wrong or if Dreiser had conveniently rewritten history so he could be the victim rather than the cause of his own problems. He wasn't likely to admit that he'd been the cause of his problems, especially not to a woman.

As I turned to leave, Dreiser said, "Wait."

When I stopped heading for the exit, Dreiser turned to the teen. "I need coffee. Something stronger than what your boss has on hand here. I take it black."

The teen jumped to his feet and slipped past us. I couldn't help noticing that Dreiser didn't offer to pay for the coffee.

He gestured for me to come all the way inside the conference room and closed the door behind me. "So, how about letting me see the interior of the house? It wouldn't take long. Fifteen minutes, tops. I'd just need to take some measurements and see how ugly the walls are. That would give me an idea of whether it's worth fighting Condor for."

"I can't do that."

"Oh, well, I had to try. Let me know if you change your mind." He handed me a crumpled business card. His craggy face didn't reveal any lingering regrets. Apparently he didn't just talk about moving on from setbacks, he actually did it. "It would be fun to snatch it out from under Condor's nose, but I'll be just as happy to wash my hands of Miriam, her house, and all of Danger Cove. I've got plenty to do before I can leave, and I'm anxious to get settled in Mexico."

I was more than happy to leave Dreiser to his preparations for paradise. He and Condor deserved each other. If there was any justice in the world, they'd *both* lose out on the chance to buy Miriam's house.

CHAPTER NINE

————

While I waited for the cab to pick me up outside Condor's building, I considered contacting Dee and Emma to let them know how intractable their landlord was. It might be better to talk to them in person, though, so I could see their reactions and judge whether they were planning something inappropriate.

They'd mentioned having an appointment at The Clip and Sip at 6:00 tonight to prepare for some kind of public appearance scheduled for tomorrow. If I met up with them at the salon, I might also be able to talk to whoever had worked on Miriam during her weekly appointments.

Until then, I should get some more work done at Miriam's house. Appraising her entire collection was going to be a full-time project for several days, and I did have other commitments next week. If my report wasn't at least close to done by the end of the coming weekend, it wouldn't be finished in time for Gil to present it at the next board of directors meeting.

I asked the cab driver to take me to Miriam's house. Once inside, I'd barely had time to take off my jacket and pull my laptop out of my quilted messenger bag when someone knocked on the front door. I didn't think it was Matt, since he couldn't possibly have run out of contacts yet for asking about local fabric-shoplifting incidents. I couldn't think of anyone else who might have been looking for me here, other than perhaps Herb Stafford, and by now Aaron Pohoke should have warned him to stay away.

It was always possible that the visitor was a friend of Miriam's who hadn't heard the sad news yet. I set my laptop on the quilting frame and peered through the front window. A tall man in business attire—shirt, tie, jacket, and khakis—stood on the front steps. He didn't so much "stand" as move restlessly, more or less in place, his steps almost too small to even qualify as baby steps. His broad smile put me in mind of a door-to-door salesman, a career that I thought was extinct even here in Danger Cove. Still, I needed to confirm he wasn't a friend of Miriam's rather than assuming the worst about him.

I opened the door a crack, and it was immediately obvious that the man wasn't surprised to see someone other than Miriam. If he'd known her, he also knew she was dead. That was a relief. I'd never been good at emotional scenes, and I wasn't sure how well I'd have handled breaking the news of Miriam's death.

"May I help you?" I opened the door a mere six inches, so I could close it again if he actually was a salesman.

His feet continued to move in tiny increments and his smile, if anything, grew even wider. "I'm Wayne Good. A friend of Miriam's. I was hoping someone would be here who could let me inside to retrieve some personal property."

It was starting to feel like everyone in town wanted to poke around Miriam's house. First Herb, then both Condor and Dreiser, and now this guy? It wasn't like Miriam had much of anything here other than quilts, which were seldom of particular interest to men unless they had huge price tags on them, which Miriam's didn't. Of course, I hadn't been inside the bedroom yet, so for all I knew, it was stacked floor to ceiling with gold bars.

"I'm sorry," I said, "but you'll need to talk to the estate's attorney. I can give you his name and number."

"I'd rather not go through all that formality." He lowered his voice and leaned closer to me. "It's kind of private, and my stuff isn't worth anything to anyone but me. Just some personal things. You know. A toothbrush, change of clothes, that sort of thing."

I felt my eyebrows rise. This was Miriam's new maybe-boyfriend? The one the mail carrier didn't trust?

If so, I could see both why Miriam would have been attracted to him and why a man might have disliked him instinctively. Wayne was in his late forties, I thought, and remarkably handsome. Not as stunning as Matt, but only another retired model could compete with his looks. Wayne Good was more of a regular guy, someone who wouldn't necessarily make everyone's head turn the way Matt did, but who might well turn the head of one friendless, poorly socialized woman unused to male attention.

"I still can't let you inside." I didn't trust him to wait outside docilely while I went to get my phone with the contact information for the estate's lawyer. "You'll have to talk to Miriam's attorney, Aaron Pohoke. His office is on Main Street. I'm sure he'd be glad to have anything of nominal value returned to you if you simply ask."

"It's just that I'd really rather this didn't become public." Despite the hint of irritation in his eyes, he chuckled in an almost-convincing display of self-consciousness. "Wouldn't want people talking about my sweet Maid Miriam."

Were there really women in this world who fell for that sort of line?

"From what I've heard, Aaron Pohoke is a good lawyer, and that means he takes confidentiality seriously. He's not going to be spreading any rumors about Ms. Stafford."

Wayne ducked his head, obviously believing he looked sheepish and endearing. Even if all my years as a lawyer hadn't hardened my heart, I'd have been more repelled than swayed by his attempt to play me.

"I have work to do," I said, starting to close the door.

"Wait." One of his restless feet lifted, and I thought he was going to stick it in the doorway to prevent me from shutting him out. He seemed to correctly read my intent to close the solid wood door whether or not his foot was there, so he set his foot back down on the porch, as if the move had merely been part of his usual restlessness. "There's one other thing. Business, not personal."

He had my attention now, and I pulled the door back open the same six inches as before. Perhaps he knew something about Miriam's quilt sales that would explain the pricing. "What business?"

"Her car." Wayne gestured over at the empty driveway. "Do you know where it is?"

"I wasn't aware that she had a car."

"Oh, yes," he said. "I sold it to her about three months ago. A solid sedan, good mileage, only one previous owner. Just right for a single lady who only drives around town."

"It sounds like you know considerably more about the vehicle than I do." It struck me that if Miriam had purchased it three months ago, that would have been only two months before she'd died. Right around the time when she'd suddenly switched to a more frequent schedule at The Clip and Sip. She'd apparently been primping for her new boyfriend. "You really should talk to the estate's attorney. If he knows about the car, he might have arranged for it to be placed in storage, and if he doesn't know, he'll appreciate the information."

"I suppose I will have to talk to him," Wayne said, trying the puppy-dog look on me again. "The loan payment's overdue. For understandable reasons, of course, but it doesn't look good to my boss. I kept telling Miriam she should arrange for automatic payments through her bank, but she always preferred to pay in cash. At first, I think it was just an excuse to see me, but it didn't take long before she realized she didn't need a reason for me to visit. All I needed was an invitation. But now, well, I wish I'd been more assertive about it. It's just that I never thought anything would happen to her. And she knew I'd never repo it from her. At least not while she needed it, but now that she's gone..."

"Mr. Pohoke can get the matter straightened out," I said firmly. "If there's nothing else, I have work to do."

"I'll talk to the attorney, but if you see him before I do, and he doesn't have the car in storage, would you tell him that Miriam's cousin probably took it?"

"Herb Stafford?"

Wayne nodded. "He's a leech. Always coming around to ask Miriam to fund some opportunity for him. Total waste of money, of course. Last I knew, he was pestering her to let him use her car. It's not like he'd ever qualify to buy his own. He came around the dealership once, wanted to buy an older model, and I ran his credit. No way he'd ever qualify for the smallest of loans, and he only had about five bucks in his bank account on a good day, when he wasn't in the red and relying on overdraft protection. Miriam always said no to his begging, but he might have taken the car when she couldn't stop him."

That was possible, I thought, since Herb had had access to Miriam's residence and had admitted to searching through the house while looking for the will. Perhaps he'd found the car keys and "borrowed" them, justifying it to himself as an advance on his inheritance. On the other hand, there hadn't been a car in the driveway either of the times I'd seen him here, so I wasn't ready to accuse Herb of anything based solely on the smarmy Wayne Good's word.

"I'll let the attorney know you stopped by, and he should expect a call from you."

"I appreciate your help." Wayne did an admirable job of disguising his sarcasm, although some of it leaked through.

I appreciated his leaving.

*　　*　　*

After another hour of inventorying Miriam's quilts—all of them as undervalued as the ones I'd viewed earlier today—I headed for Fletcher Way and the Victorian house that, a hundred years ago, had been a brothel for local lumberjacks. Now, however, it housed The Clip and Sip, a salon where customers received their choice of a homemade aperitif, a glass of wine, or a cup of espresso with their beauty services. If I hadn't known that Miriam had increased the frequency of her visits around the time she met Wayne Good, I would have thought her weekly appointments simply reflected how excellent the drinks on the menu were. I'd enjoyed several of them myself since moving to Danger Cove.

Once inside The Clip and Sip, I looked past the receptionist and caught sight of Dee and Emma in the farthest two stations. The shop's owner, Cassidi Conti, was trimming Emma's hair, and the owner's cousin, Gia Di Mitri, was standing in front of the adjoining chair, blocking my view of Dee's face.

Gia stepped back, and I could finally see what she'd been doing.

I'd never seen Dee wearing anything but very understated makeup before. Now, it was as if she'd been saving up all the products she hadn't used in the past five years in order to wear all of them today.

Gia was the first to notice my approach. She turned to say, "This is just a test run for tomorrow. What do you think? Is Ms. Madison going to be a star, or what?"

"Dee is always a star," I said honestly.

"But now she looks like one," Gia insisted. "All sparkly and everything."

"She is definitely sparkly." I turned to Dee. "What's this for?"

"Emma and I are doing story time at the library tomorrow morning."

"I'll be narrating," Emma said, "and Dee will be acting out the main character's role."

I tried to think of a children's character with that much eye makeup and came up blank. My only guess was, "Cleopatra?"

"Pre-school kids are a little too young for Shakespeare," Emma said. "No, we'll be doing *The Cat in the Hat*."

"I'm saving the whiskers until last," Gia said, stepping back so I could get another good look at her work.

Now that I knew what I was looking at, I could see that Gia had done an amazing job of making Dee's eyes look feline. And I could definitely picture Dee in a top hat.

"The kids are going to love it," I said.

"I think it needs a little more glitter," Gia said, returning to her work. "But then, doesn't everything?"

I turned to Cassidi. "I hope you don't mind my stopping by. I need to talk to Dee and Emma, and this seemed like the best time to catch them."

"That's fine," Cassidi said. "And don't mind me. A stylist never repeats what she hears from her clients."

"Never?" I said, disappointed. "I was hoping that as long as I was here, I could ask you about one of your clients, Miriam Stafford. I saw her appointment cards at her house, and I was curious if you knew why she started to come here more often in the last two months before she died."

"Miriam's death was such a shock," Cassidi said noncommittally.

"Not that big a shock," Gia said, stepping back to get a less close-up view of Dee's face. "It's not like you found the body. Not that one, anyway."

Cassidi unobtrusively nudged her cousin with her foot. "I suppose it wasn't that surprising. I had heard that Miriam wasn't in the best of health. She never complained, but it was obvious that she had trouble breathing sometimes. Every time she came in, I worried that some of the chemicals we use would set her off."

"But they didn't?" I asked.

Cassidi shook her head. "No, thank God. I don't think the salon could have survived that, not after the Barbicide incident."

I'd heard about the woman who'd turned blue and died here in the salon, but it hadn't been Cassidi's fault, so it hadn't deterred me from getting my hair cut here. It obviously hadn't deterred Miriam either.

"I understand you can't repeat anything personal that Miriam might have said, but the police don't seem to have any leads in her case, and I was thinking that maybe the change in her beauty routine meant something else had changed in her life. And if so, it might give the police some new avenues to investigate."

"I'd help if I could," Cassidi said, "but the police aren't likely to listen to any theory I have. Besides, she never said why she made more frequent appointments than before, and I didn't ask."

"It was a man," Gia said, only to get another subtle kick from her cousin. Gia turned on Cassidi. "What? It's not like it's a secret. That sort of primping is always for a man. Or a woman, I guess, if that's your thing. But Miriam was straight."

"I really don't know anything personal about Miriam." Cassidi put away her scissors and whisked the cape off Emma. "Miriam never said much about anything. Just sipped while I clipped."

"What about that last time she came in?" Gia said. "She'd been crying."

Cassidi glared at her cousin, not even trying to be subtle with her disapproval this time.

"What?" Gia asked plaintively. "Anyone could've seen that she was upset that day. She must've said something to you about why. And now she's dead. Maybe the person who made her cry her eyes out is the one who killed her. Finding him has to be more important than the freakin' stylist's code of silence."

Emma put down the hand mirror she'd been using to check the back of her head. "Keely's a lawyer. She knows all the rules about confidentiality and when you need to keep secrets and when you don't."

"I only know in the context of the attorney-client privilege," I said, "not the stylist's code."

"It doesn't matter." Cassidi absently folded the cape she'd removed from around Emma. "I really don't know anything about what happened to Miriam or why she was upset."

"Never mind," I said. "It was a long shot. I just thought that since all the local detectives are men, they might have missed the significance of the change in Miriam's beauty routine."

"I wish I did know something useful. Miriam was a good customer," Cassidi said. "If you're helping the police identify her killer, the least I can do is offer you a drink while you chat with Dee and Emma. You can all stay right here if you want, at least until my next appointment comes in fifteen minutes."

"Thanks. I'd love a decaf tea."

Cassidi and Gia disappeared, leaving me alone with Dee and Emma. I knew Cassidi was a skilled hairdresser, so it wasn't her fault, but Emma looked just the same as she always did. I was pretty sure she'd had the same haircut for the past forty years. On the other hand, Dee was completely transformed, except for the natural twinkle in her eyes, which was perfect for her role tomorrow. The kids were going to love her portrayal of the Cat in the Hat.

"Before I forget," Emma said, "we wanted to make sure you'll be at the guild's special meeting at the museum at noon on Friday. We originally scheduled it to work on a raffle quilt for the Save the Lighthouse Committee, and we'll still do that, but we're also planning to discuss what we can do about the eviction from our regular location."

"Unless, of course, you've already straightened everything out with Jack Condor," Dee said.

"He's not going to change his mind," I said. "The best I might be able to do, and I can't even promise that much, is to get you a little more time to find a new place."

"There isn't anywhere to go," Dee said.

"At least, not that we've been able to find so far," Emma said. "I've got all the quilters working their contacts, but we're coming up empty."

"What about the library?" The receptionist brought me my tea, and I glanced around to see if Cassidi's friend Amy was around. She was a librarian and might know who I could speak with there.

"Not an option," Emma said. "We've already talked to them, and they'd like to help us out, but their community room doesn't have the best lighting. Even if it suited our needs, it's solidly booked for the next year."

"With stupid stuff," Dee muttered.

"Some would call quilting stupid," I reminded her.

"They'd be wrong," Dee said firmly.

I could tell she was planning something.

"I haven't given up on finding a new meeting place for you, so don't do anything drastic without letting me know first." I didn't want to get the quilters' hopes up by mentioning that there was a chance of using the room at the museum. Gil hadn't seemed particularly optimistic about her chances of getting the board of directors to go along with it, even in the wake of a substantial inheritance from a quilter.

Meanwhile, I needed to keep Dee from making any plans that could cause more trouble than they solved while Emma and I searched for more realistic and more legal options. A distraction was called for, and I had just the thing.

"The guild's meeting space isn't the only thing I wanted to talk to you about," I said. "I had some questions about Miriam's quilting business. I haven't looked at all of her quilts yet, but so far, every single one seems to have been priced at cost, with no profit whatsoever."

"Nothing odd about that," Dee said. "I give away most of my quilts. Lots of quilters do."

"But you're not trying to earn a living," Emma said before I could. "As far as I know, the quilt sales were Miriam's only source of income."

"Are you sure she didn't have an inheritance or some sort of pension, so she didn't need to earn a living?"

The two women looked at each other, and Dee answered for them. "If she did, she never talked about it. Her parents died when she was fairly young, in her thirties, I think, and I'm pretty sure they didn't have anything to leave her. I know she worked for Frank Dreiser for a long time after that, and there's no way she'd have stuck around there if she didn't need a paycheck."

"That's what Miriam called her boss," Emma explained. "It was pretty accurate too. He scrimped and saved on everything. Which, of course, he had the right to do when it came to his own life, but not at the expense of his employees. Miriam worked for him for twenty years, and he expected her to work overtime and holidays without any extra pay."

"You should sue him," Dee said. "A class action suit. I bet everyone who ever worked for him would join it. And that's a lot of people. After Miriam left, he never could get anyone to do her job for more than a few months at a time before they quit."

"I don't sue people any longer," I reminded her.

"Right," Dee said. "You just get them arrested. So you should get Dreiser arrested."

"I'm a little busy with other matters at the moment. I've been retained to inventory Miriam's quilts."

"And now you're going to find her killer too," Dee said confidently.

"I'd really rather leave that to the police." I stood, and added the one thing that would satisfy Dee: "All I want to do when I'm not appraising Miriam's collection is to work on my first-ever quilting project. I want that pillow finished by the end of the summer."

"Good plan," Dee said. "Then you'll have time to make a wall-hanging-sized quilt for the Thanksgiving parade."

CHAPTER TEN

———

After leaving The Clip and Sip, I spent the rest of the evening practicing my appliqué stitch and doing some of the routine work involved in marketing my appraisal services. I also did a quick search online to see if I could find Miriam's virtual store. She did, indeed, have a website under the name of Miriam's Cheddar Blocks, with a gallery of quilts for sale. None of them was priced significantly above what I estimated their cost to be. I even recognized a few of the quilts from my work earlier in the day, and a quick check of my notes confirmed that the price listed on each tag was the same as what it was listed for at her website.

That pretty well ruled out the possibility that the dollar amounts on the tags were for the quilts' costs instead of their listing prices. So how had Miriam been supporting herself while only breaking even on the sale of her quilts? The only possible answers I could come up with involved criminal activity.

I woke up early the next morning, still fretting over what I was going to tell Gil about the possible taint on Miriam's quilts. I rushed through breakfast and grabbed my still-packed messenger bag on the way out the door, determined to figure out what Miriam had been up to. The most likely place to find answers was at her house.

A pickup truck was parked in Miriam's driveway. I recognized it as belonging to Alex Jordan, who'd done the work of converting a bank branch into my home. I let myself into the ranch and followed the sound of a lightly tapping hammer to the bedroom.

Considering the impact Alex had already made on Danger Cove with her painstaking restoration of a good number of historic houses, several of them in really rough shape originally, people were often surprised to find out how young she was—still in her twenties—and how small she was. She had the curves of a warrior princess, but I felt like a giant next to her, and I wasn't *that* much above the average height for a woman. She did usually dress like a contractor, though, in a work shirt that was heavy enough to ward off spring breezes coming in off the cove, plus jeans and steel-toed boots.

I couldn't actually see what she was wearing today, since all I could make out was her silhouette in the darkness of the bedroom. The windows were covered, not just with room-darkening shades, but also with thick, closed curtains. The only light in the room was a heavy-duty flashlight in Alex's hand.

She flicked it toward where I stood in the doorway, blinding me temporarily.

"Sorry," Alex said. "I wasn't expecting anyone. I guess I should have known you'd be involved as soon as I walked in the front door and saw all the quilts."

"I'm appraising them for the estate." My vision was starting to return. "What are you doing here?"

"Checking for dry rot and other hidden defects." She joined me in the better-lit hallway. "The estate's attorney asked me to take a quick look around to make sure the place was in sound condition and to write up an estimate if I thought anything was an emergency. So far, so good. For the estate, at least. I can always use a few more little jobs to keep my crew busy between the bigger, whole-house renovations."

I gestured vaguely at the darkness of the room. "What's up in there?"

"I think it's just a tripped fuse." She went back into the room to pull back the coverings that obstructed the daylight. "I just got here a few minutes ago, though."

In the sudden illumination, I could make out the details that had eluded me before. The room had been trashed. The bed coverings had been removed, down to and including the mattress cover, and then tossed haphazardly, some of them landing on a chair and the rest on the floor. The dresser drawers were either pulled out so far they were on the verge of falling or had been removed and dropped on the floor. Clothes were strewn everywhere, except along the path that Alex had forged through them on her way to the window.

"I don't suppose you did this," I said.

She shook her head. "The police, maybe?"

It was possible, but not likely. From what Fred had told me, they'd originally thought Miriam's death had been a fluke, a tragic and unexpected consequence of her lung disease. Even if they'd come back after realizing it wasn't a natural death, I couldn't see any reason why they would have undertaken such a destructive search. They would have done a thorough one, sure, leaving nothing unturned. But that would have been methodical, and this looked both random and angry.

"I don't think so." I pointed to a broken picture frame. "I've heard of police searches that were destructive, but usually when they're searching an uncooperative suspect's premises, not a victim's. Detective Marshall might not care about the mess, but I believe Bud Ohlsen's been assigned to this case, and he's a good man. He wouldn't encourage his people to damage anyone's property, and if something broke inadvertently, he wouldn't just leave it lying there."

"I've met both of the detectives." Alex pinched the bridge of her nose. "Miriam's lucky it's Ohlsen and not Marshall, or she'd never get justice."

"She may not anyway," I said. "I've heard that the police are out of leads."

"Have they talked to the neighbors to see if they'd had any disagreements with Miriam?" Alex asked as she unlocked the window and tugged it open, apparently continuing her inspection. "If not, they should talk to Dani Hudson and her husband."

"Why them in particular?"

"They wanted me to do some work on their house to get it ready to sell." Alex paused to get a closer look at something near the window's lock. Apparently it wasn't a significant problem, since she moved on from that spot and resumed talking. "That was a couple of years ago now. They didn't accept my bid, and I was just as glad. Dani's nice enough, but the husband, not so much. I heard later that they'd run into a title problem. Something to do with sideline requirements. Their foundation is just a few feet too close to the line between their yard and Miriam's. They can't sell until that's resolved."

"That sort of title issue can usually be fixed pretty easily if the two property owners are willing to work together. I got the impression that Dani and Miriam were, if not actual friends, at least not enemies."

"I think Dani and Miriam could have worked out a deal, but Lou Hudson is a loose cannon with a nasty temper. Beyond that, I can't explain it, but he just set my nerves on edge." Alex shivered. "If Miriam felt the same way, she could have refused to have anything to do with him. I did hear that Miriam had been close to signing some papers to resolve the matter, and then changed her mind at the last minute. That must have happened a month or two ago."

"And now she's dead," I said, thinking out loud. "I wonder how that's going to affect the Hudsons' prospects for selling their house."

"It can't make the prospects any worse than having to go through the legal process of getting a variance," Alex said. "I've done that a few times, and it takes forever. Plus, you never know when someone on the board will get some weird bee in his bonnet and either vote against the variance altogether or convince the rest of the board to impose some bizarre condition on it."

I nodded. "It might well be easier to get the estate's representative to sign off on the title documents than to get a variance. Especially if the representative is someone who isn't emotionally involved, like an attorney who would be used to dealing with annoying people like Mr. Hudson. Although, they might have thought they'd be dealing with Miriam's cousin, and from what I've seen of him, he'd be less cooperative than Miriam was."

Alex had worked her way around to what must have been her starting point in the bedroom. She turned off the flashlight and came out of the bedroom, closing the door behind her. She headed in the direction of the sewing room, with me following. "Poor Miriam. The owner of Some Enchanted Florist told me that he felt bad for her. No one other than the quilt guild ordered any flowers for her funeral, so he sent a couple of arrangements anonymously."

I wasn't surprised. I'd heard that George Fontaine was as generous as he was skilled at floral arrangements.

Alex stopped in the doorway, taking in the sewing room. "Interesting."

"What?" I tried to see what a contractor might find interesting about it. Probably something to do with structural integrity. Or possibly the fact that, unlike the ransacked bedroom, everything in here was tidy, with not a single piece of fabric or sewing notion so much as a quarter of an inch out of place. "You mean the lack of carnage in here?"

"That too." She used her hammer to point at the cubbies filled with fabric. "But I was more struck by Miriam's preferred color palette. I've done a lot of remodels, and I've spent quite a few hours with my grandmother looking at the quilting fabrics at Sunny Patches, but I've never known *anyone* who liked orange this much."

* * *

After a couple of hours hunched over Miriam's quilts and my laptop, I needed to stretch a bit. It was early for lunch, but if I walked over to the Teriyaki House on Main Street now, it would save me some time later.

On my way back to Miriam's neighborhood half an hour later, I felt refreshed enough to tackle the next stack of orange quilts. The novelty of cheddar had definitely worn off though.

I'd just passed Dani's driveway when she came running out of her house, the excess fabric of her muumuu—this one a lovely teal color that would tempt quilters even more than yesterday's would—flapping in her wake. She waved and called my name, so I stopped to wait for her.

"I was hoping I'd catch you," she said, sounding slightly winded from her dash out of the house. "I talked to the lawyer for the estate yesterday, and I didn't understand half of what he said. Do you know if he's going to cooperate with us to fix the title issue so we can sell our house?"

"I'm not really involved in that part of the work."

"But you're a lawyer, right?" Dani said. "So you'd understand how it works. It's really a simple deal. All the estate has to do is sign a deed giving us a few extra feet of land on the side where our garage is too close to the line, and we'll give the estate an equal amount from the corner of our back yard. It's not like there's any advantage to the estate in making us take down the whole garage, is there?"

"I can't speak for Mr. Pohoke, but I would expect him to do what's fair without being vindictive." If anyone was going to be irrational about it, it was more likely to be Dani's husband if Alex had been correct about who was responsible for the previous negotiations with Miriam falling apart. "If the fix is that simple, why didn't you work out a deal with Miriam?"

"We did." Dani wrapped her arms around her ribs, gathering the excess fabric of her dress against her. "Except right after our lawyer gave us the papers for her to sign, she met that horrible, sneaky used car salesman. He convinced Miriam to let him take over the negotiations, and he wasn't satisfied with an equal swap of land. He wanted a cash payment too. I'm pretty sure he meant to pocket it as his commission for doing the negotiations."

"At least you can be sure that Aaron Pohoke won't do anything underhanded like that. He's got a solid reputation."

"I suppose." Dani sighed and relaxed her grip on her ribs, letting her dress drape normally. "He has to be better than that awful Wayne Good. He isn't even a good used car salesman. He claimed to like Miriam personally, as a friend, not just as a customer, and he still sold her a lemon. She had to call AAA at least once a week to start it or tow it back to the dealer."

"Do you remember when you last saw it outside her house?"

"I'm afraid I didn't pay much attention to it." Dani's head turned toward the empty driveway and then back to me. "There are some shrubs that create kind of a blind spot in my view of Miriam's house, right where a garage would be. I'd even forgotten she hadn't added on to her house like almost everyone else here has. This subdivision was built for workers in the sardine cannery way back in the early 1900s. Hardly anyone had cars then, so there was no point in including garages in the original designs. We added ours shortly after we bought the house. Most of the other neighbors did too, but apparently their builders were better than ours at measuring twice and pouring the foundation once."

"What about the day Miriam died?" I asked. "Was the car in her driveway then?"

Dani's elfin face scrunched up thoughtfully. After a moment, her face relaxed and she shook her head. "If it was, I didn't see. It would have been in my blind spot. I can tell you one thing though. The driveway was definitely empty the day her body was discovered. I came over to the fence to see what was going on. I remember the ambulance backed all the way into her driveway and blocked my view of the body being wheeled out of the house. It couldn't have done that if her car was here."

So, either the car had, indeed, been at some repair shop when she died or someone had taken it between the time of her death and the discovery of her body.

"If it's missing," Dani said, "my guess would be that the used car salesman took it back. I never did trust him. My husband was so desperate to sell this house that he wanted to give in and pay the ransom, but then Wayne went too far with his demands. I don't get mad very often or very easily, but when I do, watch out! It wasn't enough that he was taking advantage of us, but then he had to go and start talking about how his 'poor, sweet Maid Miriam' didn't know how to handle money."

"He might have been right about that," I said. "Some of her business records suggest she may not have had much of a head for figures."

"Then you need to take another look at those records." Dani tugged on her dress as if it were to blame for her irritation. "She wasn't very good with people, but she was brilliant with numbers. She studied to become a CPA, you know. She got her degree and was preparing for the licensing exam when she started working for Frank Dreiser. He killed her career. She registered for the exam once, and he made her work that day so she would miss it. After that, he just wore her down by telling her how stupid she was. Which was a lie. I saw what she could do with numbers. She helped me out once when the town over-valued most of the houses on this street for tax purposes, and I had to file for an abatement. She did all the paperwork for everyone on the street, and we just had to sign it and bring it to town hall. Every single one of us got the adjustment we asked for too."

The more I learned about Miriam, the more my worst-case scenarios about her quilt business seemed to be borne out. I couldn't put off talking to Gil much longer. If Miriam's quilts had been part of some criminal scheme, the museum wouldn't want anything to do with them.

* * *

I deposited my takeout bag on the kitchen counter and shrugged out of my jacket before returning to Miriam's sewing room, although I was running out of hope that I'd find the answers I really wanted there. I'd seen enough of the quilts and their price tags to be reasonably certain that all of them were going to turn out to have been underpriced, but I still needed to complete the inventory.

I was pulling out the first of the remaining quilts—a traditional leaf block in greens and golds, alternating with cheddar setting squares—when I heard a thump that seemed to come from Miriam's bedroom. For a moment I thought Alex might have returned, but then I remembered her truck hadn't been in the driveway when I'd been talking to Dani.

Was it just my imagination, or was there someone in the house?

My stomach roiled. I let go of the leaf quilt and held onto the shelving to steady myself, anticipating the lightheadedness that followed nausea. Unconsciousness wouldn't be far behind unless I managed to get the anxiety under control.

I hadn't seen any vehicles parked on the street near Miriam's house when I returned, and the front door had been as securely closed and locked as when I'd left it. I hadn't thought to check the back door or windows, though.

I took several deep breaths, but the nausea refused to go away. If anything, it was getting worse, suggesting my subconscious had picked up on other clues that I was in danger.

I reached for the jacket pocket where I kept my phone close at hand in case of emergencies, only to remember I'd left it in the kitchen.

I was debating whether I should make a run for it, and if so, whether I had time to grab my quilted messenger bag on my way out when I heard what could only be a stealthy footstep in the hallway. My back was to the sewing room's door, and even as I whirled to face it, it slammed shut.

Through the door came a robotic voice, presumably from a text-to-speech app on the intruder's phone. "Stay in there, and you won't get hurt. I'm leaving. Count to one hundred before you come out."

I was too dizzy to concentrate on numbers, so I listened for indications the intruder had left. I heard nothing, although I wasn't sure if that was because the beating of my heart drowned out the sound, or if the intruder was waiting outside the sewing room door until he was convinced I would follow his instructions.

I wasn't in any condition to tackle him physically, but if I were convinced he was on his way out, I might consider following him stealthily. Not to stop him from leaving, just to get a good enough look at him to be able to describe him to the police. Otherwise, I had nothing useful for them to follow up on.

I continued to take slow, deep breaths, which weren't settling either the nausea or the lightheadedness, but they did keep me from losing consciousness. During one long exhalation, I heard the front door slam shut.

The rush of relief lasted only a second, replaced by anger that I'd been threatened. If I raced out to the living room now, the big picture window there might allow me to see the intruder from a safe location before he got away.

I took a step toward the door, reached for the knob, and promptly passed out.

CHAPTER ELEVEN

————

The trick to recovering from unconsciousness, as I'd learned through too much practice, was to resist the urge to immediately jump to my feet.

My doctor insisted I was fortunate that my overloaded nervous system only caused me to take a brief nap. Some people reacted to stress with seizures, strokes, or heart attacks. I didn't *feel* fortunate though. I felt frustrated that I couldn't go after the intruder on the off chance he was still visible from the front window. I had to move slowly until I was certain my nervous system had settled down, or else I'd just pass out again.

I wiggled my toes and fingers, then feet, legs and arms. When they all appeared to be in working condition and there were no sharp pains that would indicate a sprain or broken bone, I got cautiously to my feet. I jogged out of the sewing room and down the hallway to where I could see out the front window, but there was no one in sight.

I returned to the kitchen to collect my phone and dial 9-1-1. I hesitated on the verge of dialing, aware that I couldn't be sure the intrusion had been anything other than a random break-in, something that needed to be reported, but didn't rise to the level of an emergency. I'd read quite a few news stories about homes being robbed during the owner's funeral. But Miriam's final services must have happened some time ago, and the house had been unoccupied for three weeks, so why would a burglar wait so long? And why would he—or she—disguise her voice, unless it was someone I could identify?

No, I'd met too many people interested in the inside of Miriam's house—from Herb Stafford and Wayne Good to Jack

Condor and Frank Dreiser—to believe this break-in had been random.

Whatever they were all looking for, it might be related to Miriam's death, so the police needed to know about it. It also needed to be found and removed from the house for safekeeping.

Instead of dialing 9-1-1, I called Detective Ohlsen, who said he'd be right over with a forensics team. Then I called Aaron Pohoke, but his receptionist said he was in court. I left a message, asking him to call me back.

Clearly, it wasn't safe for me to be here until the police sorted everything out, and I couldn't take the quilts with me until they'd followed up on the break-in. The remainder of the inventory was going to have to wait.

I headed back to the sewing room to get my messenger bag. On the way, I passed the door to Miriam's bedroom, which was ajar. I knew better than to touch anything in case the intruder had left any evidence of his visit in there. I glanced inside, though. The curtains were still drawn back from when Alex Jordan had been in there this morning, providing enough light to see the contents of the room. It had been such a jumbled mess this morning, I couldn't tell exactly how much searching the intruder had done. One thing I did remember distinctly: at least two drawers had been dangling precariously from the dresser. Now they were lying on the floor.

The sound of a car backfiring startled me, reminding me that I needed to get out of there before anyone else came searching for whatever holy grail they thought was hidden in Miriam's home.

* * *

Bud Ohlsen arrived with wannabe-detective Officer Richie Faria in tow, along with two forensic technicians. Richie gave me a look that clearly meant *Not you, again.*

Ohlsen was more discreet and listened intently to my explanation of what had happened. There were quite a few long silences after I'd answered a question, and he mulled it over before asking me for additional details. I didn't take it personally; that was just how he worked, concentrating intently for long moments without any regard for social niceties. It was hard to read Ohlsen's expressions, but I thought he wasn't entirely convinced the intruder was related to the murder. His willingness to take me even a little seriously suggested he was desperate for leads in Miriam's death.

When I was done with my statement, Ohlsen confirmed that it hadn't been his people who'd tossed Miriam's bedroom. He also told me to stay away from Miriam's house for the rest of the day so his team could take a look at the tossed bedroom and check for new fingerprints on the doorknobs. I warned him that he'd probably find Alex Jordan's prints on the bedroom door, but that she'd been there for legitimate purposes.

With nothing more I could do on the inventory for the time being, I decided it was time to have a talk with Gil at the museum. In the lobby, the ticket-taker, Liz, set aside her e-reader just long enough to send me upstairs and call Gil to let her know I was on my way.

Gil was waiting for me in the door to her office suite. As she led me inside, she said, "You look tired. Did you pull an all-nighter to get the inventory done?" She sang a bit of "Rock Around the Clock," substituting "work" for "rock."

Her voice was so lovely I hated to cut her off with my bad news, so I waited for her to finish. When she did, she added, "I only have a minute to talk, because I was just about to head on over to the office of one of the board members. I think he might back me on hosting the quilt guild's meetings here, especially if I can give him some good news about Miriam's quilts."

"All I've got is bad news," I said. "The inventory is far from done, and I've run into a snag."

"I know this is a big project and you do have other clients," Gil said. "I'm sure you'll get it done as soon as your schedule allows."

"It's not my schedule that's the main problem." I'd thought about simply packing up all the quilts, but it would take too long. I'd still need to supervise their removal, and I'd never get both the transporting and the appraisals done before I had to stop to work on other commitments. That meant working on them solely at Miriam's house.

I explained about my safety concerns after today's experience with the intruder.

"I don't blame you for not wanting to go back there alone," Gil said. "What if I could get one of my security guards to go with you? I can see if any of them would like to work some extra hours."

I didn't know a polite way of saying that none of the museum's security guards looked sufficiently menacing to scare off an intruder. They were good at their job, but it mostly consisted of polite warnings to visitors who were naturally inclined to respect the museum's displays, or they wouldn't have been at the museum in the first place. It wasn't like the Danger Cove Historical Museum had a collection of Renaissance paintings or crown jewels that might attract dangerous criminals. Just having someone wandering the museum's halls was enough to deter any mischief here. I didn't think that would be enough for anyone who went to Miriam's house with the specific intent of committing mayhem.

"The museum shouldn't have to bear the cost of my safety at Miriam's house," I said. "That should be the estate's responsibility. I've got a call in to the attorney, and perhaps he can arrange something. In fact, he has an intern who might be able to be my escort. He's young, but he's a wrestler, and even from a distance, he looks strong. No one would want to tangle with him."

"Leave it to me," Gil said. "I'll talk to Mr. Pohoke about the break-in, and if he can't arrange for this intern to go with you, I'll find someone else."

"Thanks. I can go back tomorrow morning if there's someone available then."

"I'll make sure there is." Gil stood, preparing to leave for her meeting.

"As long as I've already ruined your day, I might as well warn you that the bequest to the museum may not be an unmitigated blessing. I've looked at enough of the quilts to know that there's something really odd about her sales. I still need to check her computer records, but if I'm right, she was selling her quilts for barely enough to cover her costs. The only way she could have been making enough of a profit for her to live on is if she was doing something illegal. You might not want the museum associated with whatever she was doing."

Gil sighed and dropped back into her chair. "Until I met you, I thought the quilting world was a lot less cutthroat than the museum world. What on earth could Miriam have been doing that was illegal?"

I shrugged. "Any number of things. The quilt sales could have been a front for something else. Or she could have been stealing the supplies to make her quilts. Or possibly some sort of fraud, selling the same quilt multiple times and telling the various buyers that it was lost in shipping or something."

Gil hummed a few bluesy notes. "It does seem like every time something good happens for the museum, there's an unsavory aspect to it too. I guess I'll just have to wait and see what your final report has to say. Then we can decide whether to decline the bequest. Unless you think I need to decide right away."

"I'm not a probate expert," I said, "but I believe you have at least a few months from the date of death to act. I'm still hoping there's some perfectly legal explanation for how Miriam could be making a living with her quilts."

"I definitely don't want the museum to be dealing in stolen goods, even if it's just indirectly."

"None of this makes sense," I said. "Aaron Pohoke told me that Miriam was a stickler for reporting her income religiously. Otherwise, I would have suspected her of tax fraud, rather than some other crime. It's possible that the list price was just for the IRS, and she was charging more than that somehow, but I'm not sure how she'd let her customers know what the real price is. Besides, it's not easy to avoid an evidence trail in an online setting, where it's not a cash business."

"One thing I learned in business school is that there's always a way around the law if you work hard enough at it. Some of the cheaters get caught, and the rest are either geniuses or lucky, benefitting from the fact that we don't live in a police state."

"I'm told that Miriam was quite bright, but it's hard to imagine her as some sort of criminal mastermind," I said. "And she definitely wasn't lucky. Not when she ended up getting smothered to death with her own quilts."

* * *

Shortly after I got home and kicked off my shoes, my phone pinged with a text from Gil. She'd arranged for Craig Pitts to meet me at Miriam's house at 10:00 the next morning, so I could resume my work there without worrying about intruders.

For the rest of the day, I used my enforced break from the inventory to review my notes, hoping to find something that I'd missed that would explain their too-low prices. I also went online to do some more research into the buyers and sellers of cheddar quilts. There were several blog posts, a Pinterest page, and even an online forum solely dedicated to this tiny niche. Miriam had been active at the forum, and it appeared that she had some dedicated followers among the pool of people who collected cheddar quilts. She'd been asked a few times about making quilts on commission, and she'd referred those people to the private message system, which I couldn't access without her password.

I wished I knew if she'd agreed to the commissions. If she had, it might explain a lot about her finances. The commissions might have been where her real income came from. Just like customers for tailor-made clothes, cheddar quilt collectors could have been willing to pay substantially more for custom work than for what amounted to off-the-rack quilts. If Miriam did accept commissions, then the other quilts she sold were comparable to samples in a portfolio rather than a product that would actually be sold.

I called Aaron Pohoke to see if he'd had any success in getting copies of Miriam's computer files, but he said it would be at least another week before all the red tape was unwound enough for him to have them. I also found out that Aaron hadn't known that Miriam had owned a car or that it was missing.

The next morning, I was tempted to head over to Miriam's house as soon as I'd finished breakfast, hoping to make up for lost time, but I forced myself to do some tidying of the vault's contents until I could be confident that Craig would be there before me. I'd almost reached the Hudsons' yard when the mail carrier, Tony Flores, joined me on the sidewalk, his huge mail bag even more stuffed than the last time I'd seen it.

"I heard about the intruder yesterday," he said, walking with me. "Are you sure it's safe to be in Miriam's house all alone?"

"I'll have someone watching my back." I pointed to where Craig Pitts was seated on the front porch, assembling a stack of cardboard flats into packing boxes. The old but pristinely maintained pickup parked in Miriam's driveway must have belonged to Craig.

Tony slapped his hand to the left side of his chest and made an exaggerated expression of despair. "Oh, no. I thought I was the only one for you."

"You are," I said. "I promise not to buy stamps from anyone but you."

"Well, that's a relief." He abandoned his pose of despair and dug into his overflowing mail pouch. "I've got a package for Miriam. I think she had some subscription services for her quilt supplies, and they probably haven't been notified yet that she passed. Do you know what the estate wants me to do with her mail?"

"I don't, but if you want to give me the package, I'll ask Craig to take it to his office. He works for the estate's attorney."

Tony reached into a side section of his bag and pulled out a packet printed with the post office's logo. "Give him this too, please. It's got everything the attorney needs to request that the mail be forwarded to his office."

I took it from him. "How did you know about the intruder, anyway?"

He shrugged. "I run into people on my route. I like to listen, and they like to talk, especially when something out of the ordinary has happened. Someone who lives nearby heard it from the spouse of a police officer, I think. She was worried that the neighborhood was becoming dangerous, what with all of the recent police involvement."

"Two incidents aren't a lot," I said. "Although I suppose when one of them is murder, it's worrisome."

"There's been more than two incidents, without even counting the ones that didn't get reported to the police," Tony said. "I can't recall all of them, but I do know her ex-boss, Frank Dreiser, made a big scene here a couple of months ago. I told Miriam she should get a restraining order against him, but she wouldn't. She said it had all been a misunderstanding, and she was certain he wouldn't be back."

"Frank Dreiser was at Miriam's house recently?"

"Oh, yes," he said. "At least twice that I know of. The first time I saw him here, he couldn't get her to answer the door. I checked on her after he left, and she told me who he was and that she didn't want anything to do with him. The second time, I'm not sure how he convinced her to open her door, but he managed it. They were shouting at each other, and I really thought he was going to push his way into her house, so I ran over to see if I could calm things down."

"Did you?"

"Eventually." Tony grinned, but it seemed forced for once. "No one—man, woman or child—can resist my charms."

"No one?" I asked skeptically.

"Okay, almost no one." He tugged his mail sack to one side, revealing a can of pepper spray affixed to his belt. "And the few exceptions fall into line when they see this." He leaned forward to whisper confidentially. "Good thing they don't know it's empty, huh?"

"Did you tell the police about Miriam's argument with her boss?"

"They didn't ask the day they found Miriam's body, and I was too upset at the time to think to mention it." Tony let his bag fall back into place, covering his pepper spray. "Do you think I should tell them now?"

"It might help," I said. "They don't have any leads, as far as I know. Detective Ohlsen is working on the case, if you want to ask for him."

"I will. Although it will have to wait until I'm done with my route." His briefly solemn tone changed back to his usual cheerfulness when he added, "After all, if snow, rain, heat, and gloom of night can't keep me from my appointed rounds, then neither can a murder investigation."

* * *

As I neared the porch, Craig asked, "What did the mail carrier want?"

I held out the package and the mail-forwarding packet. "To give me these. Would you mind taking them back to the law office with you?"

"Whatever you want," he said. "Aaron told me to consider you my boss until everything's packed up and secured."

"Packed up?"

"Yeah." Craig moved out of my way so I could come up the front steps. "Didn't he tell you? He wants me to pack up the quilts you're done with and put them in storage. And anything else you think is valuable. He's even paying me extra for the use of my truck."

"Where will he be storing the quilts? Textiles are more delicate than most people believe." If I hadn't already found another use for the bank vault in my home, I might have offered to store the quilts there. It would have been perfect: climate-controlled and completely protected from sunlight. As it was, I didn't have room for more than two or three quilts in there now, nowhere near the number in Miriam's collection. Besides, the way I used the space revealed a little too much about me personally, so I wasn't comfortable with the idea of inviting anyone other than close friends to see it.

Craig shrugged. "Aaron just told me to get the quilts to his office, and whatever he says, that's what I do. I just wish he had more work for me to do. The job's going to look great on my resume, and he pays a decent hourly rate, but it's only part-time. I'm still going to have to do my landscaping work this summer if I want to have enough money to start college in the fall. My Mom's worked hard to give me opportunities she never had, but she can't help much with my tuition."

I unlocked the door and propped it open so Craig could bring the boxes inside.

"Oh, wait," Craig said. "There was something else I was supposed to tell you. Aaron said that under no circumstances should you let Herb Stafford into Miriam's house. The guy has hired his own attorney and filed to contest the will. I bet he wouldn't do that if you were representing the estate."

I shook my head. "That was never my specialty, and even if it had been, it sounds like Herb's not being rational about his decision to sue, so it wouldn't matter who the attorney is. Even if he wins his case, the contents of Miriam's house are likely to be worth less than the cost of the lawsuit."

"I didn't tell you the best part," Craig said. "Herb didn't hire a local lawyer. It's someone from a big Seattle firm. Aaron didn't tell me the name, but it could be someone you know. I wonder if they're looking for any interns. Perhaps you could put in a good word for me."

He definitely had the persistence required of an effective attorney. "Maybe after I've observed more of your work."

"Thanks." He got to his feet and followed me inside.

I retrieved a pair of disposable latex gloves from my messenger bag and handed them to him. "You should wear these while you pack up the quilts. You can start with the ones in the living room since I've already inventoried them."

He pulled on the gloves, and I left him to the task while I went to the sewing room and picked up where I'd left off the previous day. A little while later, I got a text from Matt, saying he was at the front door, and my bouncer wouldn't let him into the club.

CHAPTER TWELVE

———

On my way to rescue Matt, I noticed that most of the living room quilts had been boxed up. The top flaps hadn't been sealed yet, so I peeked inside one. Craig had been doing his work diligently, refolding the quilts so that they fit comfortably, not simply rolling them up and stuffing them inside. That boded well for his legal career, where taking shortcuts too often got lawyers into trouble.

Craig was gushing about how his mother would never believe he'd met someone so famous, but he still refused to let Matt inside. Matt offered to let Craig take a selfie of them together, but apparently Mrs. Pitts was not a particularly trusting person and would assume it had been photoshopped.

"You can let him in," I told Craig. "Matt's here to help."

For a moment, I thought Craig was going to protest that he was all the help I needed, but apparently he had the good sense to know when persistence and eagerness went over the line to harassment. He silently stepped back to let Matt in and went straight back to his packing.

I was fairly certain that Matt was here to let me know if he'd found any evidence that Miriam had been shoplifting her supplies. That information might be a little too juicy for someone as young as Craig to resist the temptation to share it, so I didn't ask Matt for an immediate report while we walked down the hallway. Matt seemed to have picked up on my caution, because he held off saying anything until we reached the sewing room and I closed the door behind us.

"I'm glad you brought the bouncer with you," Matt said, keeping his voice low even though we were out of casual hearing range. "The more I look into Miriam's death, the more I don't think it's safe for you to be here alone."

I settled at the worktable where I'd left my laptop. "I doubt anyone would hurt me simply because I figured out Miriam had been stealing her supplies. Or whatever she was doing. She's dead, so she can't be charged with a crime."

"She might have had a partner though, and he could still get into trouble," Matt said.

"So she had been stealing her supplies?"

"Whatever she was up to, it wasn't that. No one around here had any significant problems with shoplifting of fabric, at least not to the extent that would have been needed for all of this." Matt gestured at the wall of fabric. "That's why I've been thinking Miriam might have had a partner in crime, someone who would roam farther afield to steal the supplies."

"I can't imagine who might have worked with her," I said. "I'm told she was something of a hermit. She hardly ever had any visitors, spent most of her time right here at home, and hardly talked to anyone other than the mail carrier."

"I'd heard the same thing, so I figured the best bet would be family." Matt patted his many cargo pants pockets until he came up with his notebook. He didn't actually open it, just held it ready if he needed to refer to his notes. "Miriam's cousin isn't exactly a model citizen. He doesn't stick with a job for more than a few months. That's not so unusual for a short-order cook, but in his case he's been fired more often than he's quit for a better job. He worked at the Smugglers' Tavern for a while, but it was too long ago to get any reliable information on why he left. I talked to the owner there, but Hope Foster only took over the place recently, so she never met Herb. She checked, but there was no record of him being an employee of the owner before her either. I did talk to one of Herb's current co-workers, and he said Herb had been bragging for months that he was making plans to start his own restaurant. Herb wouldn't say where he was getting the money for it though, and he certainly couldn't have financed it on his salary."

"Wayne Good claimed that Herb was always asking Miriam for money, and she was always turning him down," I said. "That doesn't sound like they were working together. But it does sound like someone with a motive to kill his only living relative. I can't even figure out how she produced enough income for her own needs, so I can't imagine she had enough extra to finance a restaurant. At least not as long as she controlled the purse strings. Once she was dead though, and this house could be sold, the proceeds would go a long way toward starting a modest business."

"Herb should definitely be a 'person of interest' in the murder investigation," Matt said, tucking away his notebook "The only thing is, he seems to have an alibi. I talked to a colleague who's working on a story about the murder investigation. Miriam's time of death was between 4:00 p.m. and 9:00 p.m. Herb worked the dinner shift that night, so he'd have been at work by 4:00 and didn't leave until well after midnight. And it's too far for him to have made the round-trip here during a break. I don't know if the police were able to confirm the alibi beyond any doubt, but presumably there are payroll records to show that Herb was at work."

"I wonder how certain they are about the time of death," I said. "From what the mail carrier said she must have been dead for more than a day before the police found her. If they're off by an hour or two on the time of death, then maybe Herb could have killed Miriam and still gotten back in time for his shift."

"Except apparently Herb doesn't have a car." Matt sat on the edge of the worktable next to my chair. "His co-worker said he was frequently late for his shifts, blaming it on delays in the public transportation."

"He might not have owned a car, but he could have had access to one shortly before Miriam died," I said. "Her car seems to have been missing since before the body was found. Wayne told me Herb had asked to borrow it. Miriam might have given him the keys before she died, and then he used the car to come kill her and get back to work on time."

"No way to know for sure," Matt said.

"And Herb's not the only one who might have taken it," I said. "Wayne Good mentioned that the loan was overdue. He acted like he didn't know where the car was, but he could have been lying, thinking it wouldn't look good to admit he'd repossessed a dead woman's property without giving the estate a chance to catch up on the debt."

"Or it could have been a random theft, someone who read her obituary and figured no one would report the car stolen for a while."

"I'd really like to know who has it," I said. "It's possible whoever killed Miriam grabbed the keys on the way out of the house."

Matt nodded. "I have some sources who might know how to find the car."

"I never thought of you as a car guy," I said, thinking of his battered pickup.

"I'm not," he said ruefully. "I do know my limits, and I'm terrible with mechanical things. It's not something I like to talk about, though. It makes me feel like too much of a cliché, the pretty boy who's afraid to get his hands dirty."

"I would never think that," I said, although it wasn't entirely true. I knew better now, but I had misjudged him initially, at least in part because of his extreme good looks, but also because he was a reporter. As a lawyer—even a retired one—I was instinctively distrustful of journalists. "But if you're not into cars, then why would you have any sources for information on missing vehicles? It doesn't seem like something that would be useful for an arts reporter."

"You'd be surprised where my work takes me. Or where I want it to take me, like inside an abandoned bank vault," he said with a grin. "I've never written about missing vehicles, but I do know some guys who use old car parts for their found-art sculptures. They'd know where the chop shops are, both legal and illegal. They probably have a source for running VIN numbers to confirm that the parts they buy are legit, and that might get us a lead on Miriam's car. It can't hurt to ask them anyway."

"Just don't get yourself arrested by an undercover officer who thinks you're trying to buy stolen parts," I said. "And before you check with your sources, I think Herb's staying at the Ocean View B&B. He doesn't seem to be the brightest guy on the planet, so if he 'borrowed' the car, it might be parked there."

"I'll try not to get myself arrested if you'll try not to get attacked by Miriam's killer."

"I'll be fine," I said. "Craig won't let anything happen to me. He's a wannabe lawyer, and he's convinced I've got the secret to being the cover story on *NWLawyer* magazine. He's going to stay within shouting distance whenever I'm here."

"Good." Matt stood and glanced around the sewing room. "I've got a bad feeling about this whole situation. Anything I can do to help here, so your work is done faster?"

"Not unless you've been certified as an appraiser since the last time we talked."

"Afraid not." He glanced in the direction of the living room as if he could see through the door and walls. "I'd offer to be your hired muscle, but you've already got that covered."

"I promise I'll be careful."

"I'll hold you to that," he said. "You owe me a visit to your vault, after all, and you can't pay up if someone succeeds in killing you first."

Despite his light tone, I thought he was truly worried about me. It was time to show him that I appreciated his concern. If I didn't commit to a specific date to show him the vault, I'd keep putting it off forever. Or until he lost interest.

The disappointment that swept over me at the thought of not seeing him again convinced me I didn't want that to happen if I could avoid it. Like he'd said earlier, sometimes a person had to take a chance and not worry excessively about the possible consequences.

"You can have your tour as soon as I finish this project."

He didn't look as pleased by my concession as I'd expected, and instead peered at me suspiciously. "I've dealt with more than my fair share of lawyers before, you know. How do you define the project? Just the inventory? Or the much bigger project of figuring out who killed Miriam?"

"You'll have your tour by the beginning of next week," I said. "The inventory report is due then, and if I don't have any leads for Detective Ohlsen by the time I finish that, I never will."

* * *

Matt opened the sewing room door to leave, and we could hear Craig's heavy footsteps heading in our direction. The hallway was too narrow for the two of them to pass side by side, so Matt turned and leaned against the wall to let Craig into the sewing room.

"Excuse me, Ms. Fairchild," Craig said, "but I've boxed up all the loose quilts. I don't know how to disconnect the one on the sewing machine setup, and I'm not sure what to do with the one on the wall. It's kind of raggedy and all, so I don't know if it's worth taking with us."

"It's definitely worth taking." In fact, it was probably worth more than all of the other quilts in the living room put together. "It's fragile, though, and the frame may be heavy. As long as Matt's still here, perhaps he'll help us with it."

We all trooped into the living room. By unspoken agreement, I supervised, and the two men did the heavy lifting. Matt and Craig each grabbed one side of the frame and, judging by the tightening of the muscles in Craig's arms, it was far heavier than it looked.

The two men looked at each other and let go of the frame. As if they'd planned it, they moved in perfect synchronization to peer between the frame and the wall on their respective sides.

Craig abandoned his inspection first and turned to look at me. "It's stuck somehow."

"Not stuck, exactly," Matt said without looking up. "I think the frame is attached directly to the wall instead of hanging from it." He ran his long, elegant fingers along where the left side of the frame touched the wall and then along the bottom and up the right side, stopping about three inches above the lower corner. He bent down to peer up at the spot where he'd stopped and then grunted triumphantly. He poked at the same spot again with his right hand and gripped the left side of the frame with his other hand. The frame swung out from the wall on a hinge.

Behind the frame was the door to what looked to me like a professional-quality safe with a digital keypad.

"Does anyone know what Miriam's birthday was?" Matt asked.

"Not me."

"If I can find out," Craig said to me, "will you give me a letter of reference for a job in Seattle?"

"I was planning to give you one anyway," I said.

"Matt too?"

Matt shrugged. "Not sure a reference from me is worth much, now that I'm just a reporter, but if you want it, sure."

"My mother *really* isn't going to believe this," Craig said as he pulled out his phone. "Give me a minute. I just have to call the office. I'm pretty sure the birth date is listed on the death certificate."

While Craig stepped out to the front porch to make the call, I asked Matt, "Do you really think that's the combination to the safe?"

He nodded. "I did a story on digital security for art collections once. Turns out that birthdays are the most common passwords for anything that requires numbers. All the instructions tell people not to use something as easily guessable as that, but I think the warning is probably counter-productive. People see the advice and even if they hadn't previously thought of using their birthday, now it's all they can think of."

Craig returned and held his phone up so Matt could read the date from the text displayed there.

Matt keyed in the numbers, but only got an error code.

"Never mind," I said. "The estate's attorney can probably contact the safe's manufacturer. They must have some kind of over-ride combination for situations like this."

Matt shook his head. "No, let me try it a little differently. I used all the digits. Miriam might have skipped the first two numbers of the year."

He tried the new combination, and there was a beep and the door opened. Matt stepped back so we could all see what was inside.

Stacks and stacks and stacks of cash.

Not neat little official bundles from the bank, but ragged piles, all different heights, and wrapped with homemade bands. I could see small, precise handwriting on the bands of the topmost bundles but couldn't read the words.

Matt, who was a little closer than Craig and I, whistled. "There must be a hundred grand in there."

CHAPTER THIRTEEN

———

Miriam's insistence on the exact wording of her bequest finally made sense to me. She hadn't been giving the museum just her quilt collection, which she had every reason to know wasn't worth all that much money. No, she'd also wanted to give the museum whatever money she had, without letting it be known that she had this much cash in her unassuming little ranch.

"Looks like Herb Stafford was right that his cousin was more than just comfortable financially," I said. "If he knew about this, it explains why he was so willing to hire an expensive lawyer to contest the will. And why it seems like everyone who knew Miriam wanted to get inside her house to search it."

Craig seemed to have been struck dumb, not a good omen for his career as a litigator where he needed to keep his wits about him, no matter what. Of course, he was young, and hadn't experienced as much as I had. After finding a couple of dead bodies, everything else was pretty minor.

Matt apparently felt the same way, because he didn't hesitate for more than a fraction of a second before asking, "You think they all suspected she had this much cash here?"

"I wouldn't be surprised," I said. "Wayne Good mentioned that she didn't trust banks. Anyone who knew her well would know that about her. They might not have known how much she had, but they would have known that any assets she had would be here, and, even better, it would be in cash, completely untraceable by anyone else who might want a piece of it."

"So what do we do now?" Matt asked.

"Normally, I'd say to leave it for the attorney to deal with, but considering how easily we were able to open the safe, I think we should pack it up and take it over to Aaron's office along with the quilts."

"He's not there, though," Craig said, finally regaining the ability to think and speak. "He's in court this morning."

"I'm sure Aaron's been paid in cash before, so he'd have a procedure in place for his staff to secure the money when he's not there."

"A few grand, sure," Craig said, still staring at the contents of the safe. "But nothing like this."

I looked at Matt. "Do you have a better idea?"

As soon as I said it, I regretted it, because I just knew he was going to mention my bank vault, and I didn't want to be responsible for the money. My new career was supposed to be low-stress, and being responsible for a hundred grand in cash was far from relaxing.

Matt paused, looking at me intently, but after a moment all he said was, "No, I think you're right. There's a box near the table where Miriam's computer used to be that I think will be the right size to hold the money."

While Craig went to get the box, I told Matt, "I'm going to the office with Craig to wait for Aaron and explain the situation."

"If you're making yourself a target with all that cash, then I'm going with you," Matt said. "Looking for Miriam's car can wait."

* * *

The quilt inventory would have to wait too, while we took care of this latest problem.

I packed up the cash while the two men finished filling boxes with the quilts that I'd reviewed and then stowing them in Craig's truck. There were still about fifty quilts left to inventory, but I could do those later today or tomorrow depending on when Aaron returned to his office.

We transported the boxes to Aaron Pohoke's office where Craig and Matt carried the quilts—not the cash, which I didn't want out of my sight until I could honestly say that I'd handed it directly to the estate's attorney—to the storage room the receptionist unlocked for us.

We were only waiting in the lobby for about ten minutes before Aaron returned from court. He greeted Matt with "No comment" and pointedly invited only me back to his office.

Aaron seemed a little distracted until I dropped the box of cash on one of the chairs facing his desk and gave him the short version of how we'd found it. "Now that you've got the money, I'll head on back to Miriam's to finish the inventory."

"Actually, if you don't mind, I need Craig to run an errand for me first. Shouldn't take more than an hour or so for him to pick up some documents at the police station. He can meet you at Miriam's after that."

As long as I couldn't get right back to work, I ought to stop by the quilt guild's special meeting at the museum. "Let's say two o'clock then."

"I'll let Craig know." Aaron finally set down the briefcase he'd been too distracted to let go of until then.

"If necessary, can Craig stay late? I'd really like to finish my initial review of the quilts today." That ought to be possible if there were no further unexpected surprises.

"I'm sure that can be arranged. If Craig can't stay the whole time, I'll find someone else to fill in." Aaron shook his head, setting the saggy skin around his neck into motion. "After all my years in practice, I should know not to expect any case to go smoothly, but I really didn't expect Miriam's estate to be anything out of the ordinary. Even after she was murdered, which can really complicate an estate, I didn't think there'd be anything else surprising about it."

"I know what you mean. In your place, I'd be spending a good bit of energy anticipating what else could possibly go wrong," I said. "Since her death, there's been at least one break-in, and now this unexplained cash. Trouble does seem to come in threes, so I have to wonder what the third thing will be."

He half-snorted and half-laughed. "Don't get me started. I don't have time for any more worries today. The judge in this morning's case just told me he wants an extensive brief prepared by first thing Monday morning, which means I'll be spending the whole weekend here at the office. This judge is known for being a bit quick to find a lawyer in contempt of court."

"I'd better let you get back to work then. I've spent a few hours in jail for contempt myself, and I wouldn't want to be the cause of it happening to you." I adjusted the strap of my messenger bag. "And I really don't want to end up in the cell beside yours."

* * *

"Are you coming with us back to Miriam's?" Matt asked as he, Craig and I trooped out of the office. "Craig offered to give me a ride so I can pick up my truck."

"I won't be going back right away," I said. "Aaron needs Craig for a couple of hours, so I'm going over to the museum. There's a guild event there, and I'm supposed to be helping them find a new place to meet, now that Jack Condor's evicting them."

"Anything I can do to help pressure him into changing his mind?" Matt asked.

I shook my head. "From what I've heard, Condor wouldn't care if you wrote a scathing article about him."

"Why don't you let them meet in your mansion?" Craig asked Matt.

"Because I don't have one," Matt said.

"My Mom said you live on a hundred-acre estate right on a lake."

"That's a bit of an exaggeration," Matt said. "In any event, I don't live the lifestyle of the rich and famous. The view is spectacular, and I enjoy a great deal of privacy, but my house is a log cabin, nothing special. Smaller than Keely's, in fact, and completely lacking in interesting features like a bank vault."

Craig turned to me. "You have a bank vault inside your house? Awesome."

"Hey, that's an idea," Matt said. "The quilt guild could meet in your vault."

"The vault isn't that big. Only about ten feet square, nowhere near enough space for the smallest of guild meetings. Three quilters would barely fit."

"I guess I'll have to take your word for it for now," Matt said. "Meanwhile, I'll ask around to see if there are any good-sized meeting spaces available. The newspaper used to have a boardroom they let nonprofit groups use, but that was before all the downsizing. We moved to new space about a year ago, and the whole office suite isn't much bigger than my house."

We reached Craig's pickup. "It's unlocked," he said as he went around to the driver-side door.

Matt paused with his hand on the passenger-side handle. "Promise you won't go back to Miriam's before your bouncer is there? Because otherwise I'm going to stick around there instead of checking on the missing car."

It was practically instinctive for me to say, "Don't worry about me," but something stopped me. Despite all the fretting I used to do on behalf of my clients, I wasn't used to anyone worrying about me. Other than my ex-paralegal, Lindsay Madison, who had become something of a mother hen after the first time I passed out, despite being a decade younger than I was.

But Matt's concern for me was different. It wasn't professional, like what I'd felt for my clients. And it wasn't even remotely paternal.

This was personal. And if Matt ever gave me a reason to worry about him, that would be personal too.

"I promise," I told him. "I'm not taking any chances this time."

*   *   *

As I watched Craig's truck leave with Matt in the passenger seat, my gaze fell on the pink and brown sign of the Cinnamon Sugar Bakery. I decided to detour over there for a snack before going to the museum. It was lunchtime, after all, I thought self-righteously, and I needed to replenish my energy if I wanted to keep from being steamrollered by Dee and Emma.

Officer Fred Fields was at the counter with his back to me.

"What's the special today?" I asked him, and he started guiltily before whirling around to face me. He probably thought for a moment that he'd been caught by his wife, who struggled heroically to get him to eat fewer sweets.

When he realized he wasn't in the doghouse, he said, "Carrot cupcakes. They're practically vegetables, right?"

"I couldn't swear to that in court."

He sighed. "I know. But I can honestly tell Sally that I had carrots at lunchtime. And I'll have extra salad with dinner tonight. I promise. It's just that…well, it's carrot cake. How can I *not* have a taste?"

I noted that the clerk was sticking not just one, but four of the cupcakes into a bag. Fortunately, I wasn't his wife or his doctor, so I didn't need to give him a lecture. "Do you know if Detective Ohlsen found anything useful at Miriam Stafford's house yesterday?"

"Nothing at all." Fred's expression held a mixture of grimness and frustration. "I was really hoping they'd get a lead. I mean, I wasn't happy that you'd been in danger, but I'm glad someone was there to notice there'd been a break-in. The thing is, if something doesn't come along to shed some light on the case soon, it never will."

"I didn't think to mention it to Ohlsen," I said, "but it looks like Miriam's car is missing. I told the attorney, but he's been busy, so he may not have passed the information along to the detective. I don't know if its disappearance is even related to her murder. It could have been borrowed or stolen before she died."

"I hadn't heard anything about that," Fred said. "I should get back to work now, but when I get a chance, I'll check with Ohlsen to see if he knows anything about Miriam's car."

"Thanks." I gave the clerk my order for a single carrot cupcake, and then thought of something else I wanted to ask Fred. I turned to catch him. "One more thing. Did you know that Jack Condor is evicting the quilt guild from their regular meeting space?"

"Yeah." Fred's face looked almost as grim as when he'd contemplated the possibility that Miriam's killer would get away with murder. "You think he had something to do with Miriam's death?"

"I wouldn't put murder past him, but I can't see any real motive for him to kill Miriam. He'd like to buy her house, but I think that's true of pretty much every piece of property in Danger Cove that he doesn't already own. No, what I was wondering was if you knew of any possible meeting space for the quilt guild."

Fred thought for a moment before shaking his head. "Too bad they couldn't meet at the lighthouse. The first lighthouse keeper was a quilter, you know."

"I do know," I said. "Her name was Maria Dolores."

"Oh, yeah," he said sheepishly. "I forgot. You helped to identify her quilt before the museum acquired it."

"Why can't the guild meet in the lighthouse?" I asked. "The quilters have certainly raised a lot of money for the Save the Lighthouse Committee, and they're not done yet."

"That's sort of the problem," Fred said. "The lighthouse has had a lot of repairs recently, but it's still not safe enough for regular use. Can't risk someone getting hurt."

"Definitely not." Having been a personal injury lawyer, I knew that the money awarded in a lawsuit was never truly enough that the client wouldn't have preferred to have avoided the injury. "So the lighthouse isn't an option. Where else could the quilters meet?"

Fred thought for a moment before shaking his head. "Nowhere I can think of. Space is at a premium in Danger Cove these days. There are some responsible developers in town, of course, but they're frequently outbid by Jack Condor who snaps up any empty space he can find and tries to squeeze every possible penny out of it, no matter what the neighbors think."

"What about Frank Dreiser?" I said. "I met him at Condor's office. Apparently he's recently decided to retire to Mexico. What kind of a developer was he?"

"Dreiser isn't as bad as Condor when it came to over-development," Fred said, turning grim again "But I will say I'm glad he won't be living here any longer. Dreiser's office was at the top of the list of businesses requiring the most frequent police interventions pretty much every year I've been on the job."

"How serious were the incidents?"

"That's the frustrating thing," Fred said. "It was hard to pin anything on Dreiser, even though we knew he was the source of the problem. The witnesses always confirmed that he never took the first swing. He might defend himself afterwards, but he always waited for someone else to throw the first punch. That way, he could claim to be the victim, even though we knew he'd provoked the other person—usually an employee or subcontractor—beyond endurance. We could have gotten creative and found a way to arrest him, but it's tricky. Usually if we charge one person in an altercation, we have to charge both of them, and what we really wanted was to get Dreiser sentenced to an anger management program. We did, eventually, although I can't say it did any good."

"When was the last time you responded to a call at his office?"

Fred brightened. "You know, I hadn't even realized it, but it's been at least a month." Then he frowned again. "If he's been holding himself in check for this long, he'll probably erupt like a volcano soon. I'd better warn everyone at the station."

"Just one more question, if you don't mind." I waited for him to nod before asking, "Was Miriam ever involved in one of those disputes with Dreiser?"

"Not that I recall," Fred said, "but, really, there were so many incidents, it's hard to be sure. The only thing that really stands out is that he always started the situation, saying or doing something inflammatory. Afterwards, he claimed he hadn't meant anything, and he was totally shocked that the other person had gotten angry. I almost believed it the first time, back when I was a rookie, but one of the more experienced officers set me straight."

Fred had been on the job for at least twenty years now. That meant that Dreiser's abusive behavior wasn't a recent phenomenon but went back into the period when Miriam had worked for him. He'd claimed that Miriam had quit for no reason, but it sounded more likely that he'd goaded her into it.

Dreiser was obviously an abusive jerk, and, much like the officers who'd wanted to arrest him for causing trouble, I really wanted to pin Miriam's murder on him. Unfortunately, since he didn't have a reputation for assault, it seemed unlikely that he would have intended to kill her. He might have taunted her, though. Perhaps thrown the quilts on top of her, saying something derogatory about them and how she'd been wasting her time making them.

That much, I could imagine, but would he have let her struggle to get the quilts off her, suffocating to death while he stood by and did nothing? Even Dreiser couldn't be deluded enough to paint himself a victim in that case.

CHAPTER FOURTEEN

———

As I climbed the stairs to the second floor of the museum, I could hear the sound of cheerful voices coming from the boardroom. I was anxious to see the raffle quilt they were making, but I had to take care of business before I could join them. Reluctantly, I turned in the other direction, toward Gil's office.

She was humming something with an emphatically morose feel to it. For once, I didn't feel bad about interrupting her mid-song.

She went silent the moment she saw me. "The way my week is going, I'm guessing there's been more trouble at Miriam's house."

"Not trouble, exactly." I dropped into a chair across from her to explain about the hidden safe and the cash.

When I was finished, she asked, "But isn't that good news? If the money was in the house, then it's part of the bequest to the museum. We can always use cash, and you said the quilts themselves aren't worth a lot of money."

"I'm probably worrying about nothing, but that's what I do." I adjusted the messenger bag on my lap. "If Miriam wasn't making enough money to live on from the sale of her quilts, then where did she get that kind of cash? She had no known assets from before she quit working for Frank Dreiser ten years ago, and since then she hasn't had a job that anyone knows about other than the quiltmaking. Given those circumstances, I can think of far more illegal sources for that money than legal ones. If I'm right, you won't want the museum to be associated with that."

"True." Gil hummed a few notes of her morose song. "In fact, the board member I spoke to yesterday didn't even like the idea of accepting a bequest from a murder victim, just in case someone might think we'd killed her for the inheritance. Which is just silly. We didn't even know Miriam had named us in the will until three weeks after she died."

"Are the rest of the board members as irrational as this one?"

"They all have their quirks," Gil said diplomatically. "I don't think any of the others have really thought about the possibility of bad PR from the bequest. They're just thrilled to have what might be a significant donation."

"Perhaps the amount of the bequest will blind most of them to the PR issues. Despite all the delays, I'm still hoping to have the inventory of Miriam's quilts finished before your next board meeting. Each quilt isn't worth much, but there are a lot of them, so they'll add up for a nice total."

"Assuming they're not tainted the same way as the money in the safe."

I wished I had as nice a voice as Gil's. Then we could have harmonized on the morose song she'd been humming earlier.

As long as I was dwelling on the bad news, I had to ask, "Did you get a chance to talk to that board member about letting the quilters use the boardroom as their regular meeting space?"

Gil shook her head. "I decided discretion was the better part of valor and didn't bring it up. If it weren't so frustrating, it would almost be funny. Most people think of quilters as sweet little old ladies, which is lazy stereotyping, of course, but this particular board member somehow got it into his head that Dee is some sort of Ma Barker, leading a gang of criminal quilters. He kept ranting about two previous murders connected to the guild and who knew what lesser crimes they might have committed?"

"If Dee led a criminal gang, Emma would make sure the bodies were never found."

"True." Gil smiled ruefully. "I'm just sorry the timing is so bad. If Miriam's murder weren't so recent, the board might be more inclined to remember all the good things associated with quilters, so I could let the guild use the boardroom for all of their meetings instead of just the special ones like today's. Although, at this rate, they may vote against letting the quilters use the boardroom at all, ever, and then my hands will be tied."

"I'm sure you won't let that happen." I stood to leave. "I'd better go see what Dee and Emma are up to. They're counting on me to take care of everything in the wake of the eviction notice, but they always have a backup plan, and trust me, you don't want to know how bad those plans usually are."

* * *

The heavy double doors of the boardroom had been propped open. When the museum had acquired the historic mercantile building from the late 1800s, the second floor had been divided into the boardroom, Gil's office suite, and two archive areas. The boardroom still had something of a warehouse feel to it, with a high ceiling, scarred wood floors, and fifteen hundred square feet of open space.

The huge conference table that seated eighteen people had been shoved against the wall across from the entrance, beneath the large windows overlooking Main Street. The chairs had been lined up along the opposite wall, just as they'd been during the ornament-making event a few months ago. Sewing machines had been set up on two banquet-sized folding tables with laminate tops, and another table held cutting boards and stacks of two-inch squares made out of two right triangles, one a dark print and the other a solid light blue.

The quilters were busy turning the pieced squares into Ocean Waves blocks, a traditional pattern that dated back to before the Danger Cove Lighthouse had been built in 1894. I'd been assured that the blocks were simple to make, but once the blocks were laid out in rows, they would create the illusion of intricately interwoven triangles surrounding large light-blue squares.

Dee was at the front table, sewing the pieced squares into blocks, while Emma circulated, politely cracking the whip over the workers. Dee's eyes no longer looked like a cat's, but apparently she'd taken a fancy to the top hat, because it was on the table to her right. She didn't notice my arrival, and I didn't want to interrupt her work just to give her bad news.

The table beneath the huge windows overlooking Main Street was filled with snacks. Probably Emma's doing, since there was nothing like free food to bring out volunteers.

I wasn't hungry, but I needed some additional hydration. When I'd left the house this morning, I'd forgotten to bring a water bottle with me, and the cup of tea I'd gulped down at the Cinnamon Sugar Bakery had barely taken the edge off my thirst.

I made my way over to the refreshments table. Faith Miller, the woman who'd demonstrated the appliqué stitch for me earlier in the week, was there, filling a small paper plate with crudités and a drizzle of dressing.

She turned to greet me. "How's your pillow top coming along?"

"Slowly," I said. "I've been distracted."

She nodded. "Finding us a new meeting place. Dee said you'd take care of it."

"Dee sometimes has more faith in me than I deserve. I hope I'm not the only person looking for your new meeting space."

"I wish I could help," Faith said, "but between homeschooling my kids and dealing with contractors on some major repairs to my house, I'm lucky to get to do anything at all with the guild. I could only be here today because another homeschooler in my network owed me a few hours from when I watched her kids last week while she was sick."

"I'm sure Dee understands. And appreciates your helping with the raffle quilts."

Faith twirled a carrot stick in the puddle of dressing on her plate. "I heard you're a lawyer as well as a quilt appraiser."

"Not any more." I grabbed a bottle of water and uncapped it. "I've retired from practicing law."

"Still, you know legal stuff, right?"

I nodded warily.

"It's just that, well, I know it's not nice to speak ill of the dead, but I can't stop thinking about how Miriam stole my quilt design. Back when I first saw what she'd done, I went to see a lawyer about my rights. He said I couldn't do anything about it, and when I asked questions, he got impatient with me, so I never got any helpful explanations."

"Copyright law is a very specialized field of law, not one that I ever studied in law school or during my practice." It had been touched on briefly in the quilt-appraisal training, and I'd done some extracurricular reading at the nearest law library, but my knowledge of the field was still limited. "I only know the basics as they relate to quilts."

"Perhaps you can explain why it's okay for Miriam—may she rest in peace—to steal my design, and there's nothing I can do about it."

"It's not okay for anyone to steal your design," I said. "The problem is that it would be very difficult and very expensive to prove."

"But I have pictures." She jabbed another carrot into the dressing.

"That wouldn't be enough, I'm afraid. Your quilt is based on a traditional block, something that isn't copyrighted. You'd have to prove that your use of that block was significantly different from what quilters have been doing with the design for centuries."

"It *is* different. Unique even," Faith said. "The way I laid out the blocks creates a secondary design. Miriam copied that part of it, too, not just the underlying block design."

"You may well be right, but there are other possible explanations that you'd have to disprove," I said. "For one thing, Miriam had an antique Robbing Peter to Pay Paul quilt hanging on her living room wall, so it's a block she obviously admires. She also has a considerable library of quilt design books, which could have inspired her. The block goes back at least to the late 1920s, if I remember correctly, possibly longer under other names. There's also such a thing in the design world as synchronicity, where multiple people have essentially the same idea all at the same time. I've seen it myself, when for no apparent reason, several quiltmakers simultaneously became fascinated with a traditional block that hadn't been used much in recent years. No one knows exactly why it happens though. Perhaps they all read the same magazines or went to the same quilt exhibit, and were inspired to hunt out the uncommon block and make similar uses of it."

"It's just not fair," Faith insisted. "I *know* Miriam flat-out copied my design. I teach my kids that if they do the right thing, then other people will do right by them. How can I even say that to them now?"

"I'm sorry." The desire to make the world a little bit more fair had been part of why I'd become a lawyer. Probably part of why I'd had to retire too. The stress of trying to overcome such an immutable fact of life as unfairness had been immense. "I wish I could offer you some hope, but it would be false."

Faith stabbed the carrot stick into the dressing again, and I half expected the point to go straight through the reinforced paper. "It's just not fair," she repeated before setting down the last of her carrot daggers and wandering off to work at an ironing station.

I couldn't help thinking that the desire for revenge wasn't always triggered by something big. It could be something very small, at least to an outsider. To the person who'd been pushed to murderous thoughts, though, the incident was either the final straw on an overburdened back or the loss of something that made it possible to cope with that overburdened back.

For Faith, quilting was the coping tool that made it possible for her to keep moving forward with raising her kids, homeschooling them, and taking care of the household chores all alone. If she lost the joy she found in quilting and then learned that she had no legal recourse against the person who'd cost her that coping tool, would she be tempted to get it back, even if it meant turning violent?

I didn't believe Faith could be so irrational that she would premeditate a murder. Most killers weren't, after all. And yet murders still happened.

What if Faith had gone to Miriam's house to confront her about the supposed design theft and then lost her temper? She could have thrown the quilts in a fit of pique, leaving before she even realized that Miriam was in any distress.

That scenario seemed a little too plausible for my peace of mind. Especially since it didn't narrow down the suspects at all. It could apply to anyone who'd been inside Miriam's house before her death. I wasn't sure that Faith had visited Miriam, but I knew at least three other people who had been inside her home: Herb Stafford, Frank Dreiser, and Wayne Good. Miriam had refused to lend Herb the money he wanted, so he definitely had a motive for wanting her dead, and Frank Dreiser had argued with her loudly enough to trigger a call to the police. I wasn't sure about Wayne, but he obviously wanted something from Miriam, and he might have turned angry if she'd rejected him.

I thought I understood the basic picture of how Miriam had ended up dead—an impulsive act that wasn't intended to have deadly consequences—but that didn't resolve the ultimate question of who had been the one to lose his temper.

Or the one to lose *her* temper, I thought, taking note of the way Faith was using her iron. She wasn't pressing gently as I'd been taught to do by a self-appointed member of the quilt police—Faith was viciously throttling her blocks.

* * *

Dee called me over to her table and offered me the empty middle chair. I declined, knowing that if I sat behind a sewing machine, Dee would insist that I actually use it. Instead, I pulled up a chair next to the end of the table, and a moment later Emma came over to take the seat I'd avoided.

"Have you found us a new meeting place?" Dee asked me.

I was as stuck with that assignment as the police were in their investigation of Miriam's murder. "I've got some feelers out, but no leads yet. You're still looking too, right?"

Emma caught my eye and nodded, so I knew that she, at least, was still actively searching for a new meeting site.

For once, though, the two women weren't in agreement. Dee shook her head and said, "We've talked to everyone who came to today's event, and no one can think of a good place for us to meet. But that's okay. We have confidence in you. You'll take care of it."

Before I could explain that her confidence was misplaced, I caught sight of Herb Stafford coming through the double doors. He stopped next to the opening and scanned the room until he caught sight of me.

He came over and said, "Hello, ladies." He nodded at Dee and Emma before turning to me. "I know we got off on the wrong foot the other day, and now you're working for the other side of the case, but you did say you could give me the name of another appraiser."

"Keely's the best," Dee snapped. "No point in getting a second opinion if hers is the first one."

"I'm just doing what my lawyer told me to do," Herb whined. "It's nothing personal."

Dee sniffed. "That's what people always say when they're doing something they know is wrong. If you respected Miriam's wishes, you wouldn't be contesting her will to start with, so you wouldn't need your own appraisal."

Once again, the Danger Cove grapevine—or maybe it was the quilters' grapevine—had shown how quickly and accurately it could spread gossip.

"I do respect Miriam's wishes," Herb said. "That's actually why I'm contesting the will. I'm sure she didn't mean to give so much of her estate to the museum. I blame the lawyer for allowing an obviously incompetent old woman to sign a will."

"Miriam was no less competent than I am," Dee said.

"She was a big help with the last quilt show," Emma added. "Miriam was in charge of scheduling all the volunteer shifts and making sure everyone showed up. She created the most amazing spreadsheet I'd ever seen."

"That's different," Herb said.

I gave him a moment to explain what, exactly, was different about preparing a complicated spreadsheet and knowing what she wanted done with her assets after she died. He remained silent, and I was running out of time before Craig would be waiting for me at Miriam's house.

"If you really want to go ahead with the will contest," I said finally, "I can give you some names of certified quilt appraisers. I have them at home and can text them to you this evening."

Herb looked at me suspiciously. "You're not just brushing me off?"

Dee snorted. "If she wanted to brush you off, you'd know it."

"It's best for both sides of a case if everyone has access to a qualified expert," I said. "It will save a lot of time and money for both sides if you don't get unrealistic expectations of the quilts' value. You should also talk to the appraiser about the expenses involved in selling the quilts. That will take a big bite out of the bottom line."

"It won't cost much if I sell the entire collection to the museum," Herb said. "I'm not really interested in the quilts. It's mostly the other stuff in the house that I'm concerned about."

Things like a hundred grand in cash? Did he know about the wall safe?

As if he'd heard my thoughts, he added, "I don't even know for sure what's in the house. It's probably only sentimental things, but Miriam would have wanted them to stay in the family, and I'm all she had. The only way to guarantee I'll get what I deserve is to contest the will."

Despite his explanation, I was more convinced than ever that Herb did know about the cash in the house. On the other hand, he couldn't possibly know that we'd found it and turned it over to Aaron already, and I wasn't going to tell him. "Miriam did leave you her house. That's got to be a pretty substantial share of the estate's value."

"I suppose," Herb said, picking at one of the stains on his T-shirt. "It's going to take time to sell it, though. My lawyer said it could be a year or more. I'm betting it will be even longer. The house next door has been on the market for at least two years now."

I couldn't help asking, "What's your hurry? Whatever you get from the estate is a windfall, not something you ever expected to get."

He shrugged. "I've got plans."

"To start your own restaurant?" I asked. "I understand that's something you've dreamed of for a while."

Surprise flashed across his face before he affected a look of indifference. "Why would I want to own my own restaurant? They're money pits. Even if Miriam's quilts were worth ten times as much as you say, they wouldn't be enough to really get a restaurant off to a good start. Besides, I make a lot more as a chef than I would as the owner. Without the stress and long workdays."

"So what do you want to do with the inheritance?"

"I thought I'd buy a boat," he said. "Maybe live on it."

From what I'd heard, owning a boat was at least as much of a money pit as owning a restaurant, without even the distant chance of ever seeing any profit.

I completely understood why Miriam would have wanted the museum to inherit the quilts. It was obvious that Herb didn't care about them, and the museum would make sure that they ended up with someone who cared about them. But why hadn't she wanted Herb to get the cash? And why had Miriam been so secretive about it, not even telling her attorney that the real value in the contents of her house wasn't in the quilts?

CHAPTER FIFTEEN

Craig Pitts was waiting for me on Miriam's front steps. We quickly settled into an efficient routine. Craig helped me spread out each quilt, and then I photographed it. While I was making notes in my laptop, Craig folded the quilt neatly and packed it into a box.

By 4:30 both of us needed a break from the cramped sewing room, and I needed a break from Craig's incessant questions about life in the big city. I called in an order to Gino's Pizzeria for pickup. Craig was reluctant to go get the sandwiches, since he didn't want to leave me at Miriam's alone. I eventually convinced him that I'd be perfectly safe, since we knew there wasn't anyone already in the house, I'd deadbolt the door behind him, and he'd only be gone about half an hour. He made me promise to keep my phone close at hand and to call 9-1-1 if anything unusual happened. He sounded like my ex-paralegal, Lindsay, except she'd been worried about my being able to call for help if I felt the warning signs of a syncope event. Craig waited until I showed him my phone at the ready before taking the money I held out for him and heading out the front door. He even paused outside on the front porch until I turned the deadbolt.

Despite myself, I was a bit nervous about returning to the sewing room where the intruder had trapped me before. At least while Craig was gone, it might be best if I stayed within sight of an exit.

There was a back door in the kitchen, so I headed there to see if I could find anything about Miriam's quilt sales that I might have missed in my initial quick flip through the stacks of papers on the table there. The first pile consisted of bills for basic living expenses like taxes, utilities, and insurance. The next one was quilting magazines that she hadn't gotten around to filing away in her sewing room. The final stack consisted of printouts of designs she'd found online and photocopies of quilt pictures from magazines. At the bottom was a three-ring binder that seemed to hold the most promise for containing business records.

I sat at the table and leafed through the pages, most of which were graph paper with clippings of quilt pictures glued to it. There were handwritten notes, mostly recording how she'd gone about making a variation on the pictured quilt. It was just the sort of journal that quilt historians would kill for, figuratively speaking. It might have been an interesting research project for someone to match these notes with the completed quilts, comparing the idea with the finished product. I wasn't the right person to do that sort of research, but I did find the notes interesting.

I was going to set the notebook aside when I remembered Faith's claim that her Robbing Peter to Pay Paul quilt had been copied by Miriam. If so, perhaps there'd be a picture of Faith's quilt in the notebook and notes about the one Miriam made from that design.

I flipped quickly through the pages, and about two-thirds of the way to the back of the notebook, I found some pictures of quilts I recognized from the most recent guild show. I slowed down then, making sure to look at each page individually.

I didn't see any Robbing Peter to Pay Paul quilts before the contents of the journal changed significantly. There were no more pictures, just graph paper filled with spreadsheets. For a moment, I thought I might have finally found some business records to shed light on her quilt sales, but my hopes were dashed by the title of the first spreadsheet: "People who made me angry."

Assuming that the anger might have been mutual, Detective Ohlsen should see this. It wasn't every day that a victim served up a list of possible suspects for her own murder.

I reached for my phone, only to change my mind. Calling Ohlsen could wait a few minutes. I couldn't take the journal to the police station until Craig returned anyway, and I doubted Ohlsen would be sufficiently impressed by my sleuthing to save me a trip by racing over here, sirens wailing and lights flashing.

The spreadsheet wouldn't help me place a value on Miriam's quilts, but I couldn't help reading it. There were three columns: name, date, and comments. The first name was Frank Dreiser's, and the date coincided with when Miriam had been working for him, and the comments section contained the note "cheated me out of overtime."

The spreadsheet continued for about twenty pages, with her various grievances listed in chronological order. In addition to Dreiser, whose entries only stopped when she quit working for him, there were quite a few mentions of Herb Stafford. It looked like he'd asked for money at roughly six-month intervals for the past ten years.

More recently, there were a few mentions of Dani Hudson, including the breakdown of their negotiations and then the phone call that had brought the police to check on the shouting at Miriam's house shortly before her death. Unfortunately, she didn't name the person she'd been arguing with that day. The very last entry was for Wayne Good, with the comment, "sold me a lemon."

I didn't recognize most of the other names, but from the comments, I could piece together that many of them were health care providers and insurers. There was even one line, dated about two weeks before she died, referring to the mail carrier, Tony Flores. In the comments, she indicated that he'd interrupted her quilting by knocking on her door to hand her a package that could have been left on the porch. Beneath that was the name of someone I inferred from the comment was Tony's supervisor, to whom she'd complained about the mail carrier's excessive zeal. Apparently the supervisor hadn't been particularly sympathetic. I wondered if Tony knew about the complaint. Considering that he'd been the only person who cared enough about Miriam to notice that she'd died, it seemed particularly sad that she hadn't appreciated him more.

One name was conspicuously absent from the spreadsheet: the quilter, Faith Miller. Of course, that didn't completely exonerate Faith. If she had killed Miriam in a rage over the purported copyright infringement, it was entirely possible that Miriam hadn't even known about Faith's suspicion until it was too late to write it in her spreadsheet. In my experience with personal injury claims, that kind of obliviousness to having wronged someone could be even more infuriating to the victim than the wrongful act itself.

I reached what appeared to be the end, with only a dozen or so lines filled in. I turned it over to confirm that there wasn't anything else of possible interest. The next page was a list, titled "I only took what I was owed," and beneath that was a list of Miriam's grievances against Dreiser. First among them was his failure to pay her for all the hours she actually worked, or to pay overtime rates when he made her come to the office on holidays. The final straw that had caused her to quit had been when he'd refused to pay her for some sick leave after her lung condition had landed her in the hospital for two weeks.

On the back of the page was a detailed chart that covered what appeared to be the entire ten years she'd worked for him, with precise calculations of the wages she'd been owed—complete with the number of hours she was shorted each month, calculated to the nearest tenth of an hour, and the relevant hourly rate—and then the amount she'd embezzled to pay herself, which was exactly enough to cover the amount she'd been cheated out of.

Now I knew where the cash in the safe deposit box had come from. And the prices on Miriam's quilts made perfect sense. She'd been using the quilt sales to launder the money she'd embezzled.

If she'd simply spent the money without having any obvious source of income, people—and the IRS—would have been suspicious. By selling the quilts at cost, though, and presumably under-reporting the expense of the materials to make them, she created both the impression that she had a source of income, and also a paper trail, if anyone wanted proof of her income. Only someone who knew the true cost of making a quilt would know that the numbers didn't add up.

I used my phone to photograph the incriminating spreadsheet as a precaution against anything happening to it before the police received it. As I worked, I reflected on how Gil was going to take the news that Miriam's quilts were definitely implicated in illegal activity. At least now Gil would know the truth in plenty of time to do whatever was necessary to protect the museum's reputation. And I could rest easy, having resolved the mystery of Miriam's underpriced quilts. I might even have found critical evidence that would eventually help the police solve her murder, probably pinning it on either Frank Dreiser or Herb Stafford, who had the strongest motives for wanting Miriam dead.

* * *

I had lost track of time while studying Miriam's notebook, so Craig's knock on the front door startled me. I carried the notebook with me as I went to let him in.

"Change in plans," I told him. "We need to go to your office. Would you mind giving me a ride?"

"Now?" he said with a plaintive glance at the big paper bag full of sandwiches and chips. "I'm starved."

"You can eat when we get there," I said. "I found something that Aaron needs to see right away. The police too."

Craig sighed. "I guess I can wait five minutes before I eat. Let's go."

"Not quite yet," I said. "I need to grab my laptop first. You can wait in the car if you want. Maybe even take a few bites of your sandwich while you're waiting."

"If you've got evidence to help catch Miriam's killer, I'm sticking close to you. I wouldn't want anything to happen to it." He tucked the takeout bag under his arm as if it were a football. "Do you want me to carry the evidence for you?"

"Thanks, but I've got it. It will fit in my bag, and it's not heavy."

Craig followed me back to the sewing room. "What is it?"

"A notebook," I said. "Miriam wrote down the names of everyone she'd ever been angry with. It's almost like she expected someone to kill her and wanted to be sure the police knew who might have argued with her."

"This is awesome," Craig said. "I never thought I'd be involved in something like this even before I became a lawyer."

"It's not always this exciting." I stuffed the notebook into my messenger bag and turned to leave the room. "Most of the work is repetitive, and there's hardly ever anything as obvious as a list of suspects prepared by the victim."

"Who's on it?" Craig said. "Anyone I might know?"

"The most likely is her ex-boss, Frank Dreiser. He had at least two hundred thousand dollars' worth of reasons to want to kill her."

Craig's eyes widened. "Two hundred grand?"

I glanced around the room to make sure I hadn't forgotten anything else I needed right away. There were only about a dozen quilts left to review, but I wasn't entirely sure when I'd be able to come back and finish them. It all depended on whether Aaron turned the notebook over to the police right away and then how Detective Ohlsen reacted to it. Since his team had missed the importance of this notebook, he might be concerned that they'd missed other useful evidence. If so, he might declare Miriam's entire house an active crime scene again, and I'd be barred from finishing my work here.

I decided there wasn't anything I could take from here quickly, other than the packing box that was about three-quarters full of quilts I'd already reviewed. I pointed to it. "If you'll take that out to the car, I can carry our lunch."

"You've got enough to deal with already," he said, pointing to my bulging messenger bag and the laptop. "I'll just put the bag inside the box."

"Wait." I upended a large plastic bag that was full of fabric from a recent shopping trip. "Put the food bag inside this one, so there's no chance of a greasy leak onto the quilts."

Craig did as I instructed and then hefted the large packing box. I followed him to the front door, holding it open and then staying behind to lock it while he trotted over to his truck. He was tossing it into the back of the truck when I heard what sounded like a moan coming from behind Miriam's house. My stomach immediately churned, producing a few tendrils of nausea, just enough to confirm that I hadn't imagined the sound.

I glanced at Craig, but he was moving something out of the way of the box full of quilts so there was no risk of it falling out as we drove. He didn't seem to have heard the low sound of distress, but I was confident he was close enough to hear me shout if I needed help.

I followed the side of the house to the back corner and peered around it. Crumpled on the ground, a mere foot or so past the corner was Tony Flores.

The huge messenger bag that almost seemed a part of him was missing, his eyes were closed, and his usually animated face was slack. I thought I saw some blood on the grass near his head.

I'd been right to anticipate a third disaster for Miriam's estate. I just hadn't expected it to be yet another murderous attack.

CHAPTER SIXTEEN

I pulled out my phone to dial 9-1-1 and shouted for Craig. He arrived at a gallop just as I was telling the dispatcher that a man had been injured and was unconscious. I gave the address and then sent Craig out to the street to meet the first responders and lead them out back.

Tony wasn't moving, and I was afraid the moan I'd heard had been his dying breath. I set my laptop and messenger bag down a safe distance from the body and knelt to check his pulse. I was relieved to find that he had one, although it seemed faint and erratic to me. Of course, all I knew about medical matters came from reading medical reports to prepare for trial, and that was a lot different from hands-on experience with an injured person.

I sat on the lawn beside Tony, taking his hand in case it would help him to know, even while unconscious, that he wasn't alone and help was on the way.

Who could possibly have wanted to hurt Tony? He was such a cheerful, caring person, dedicated to his work and the people on his route. It had to be related to Miriam's death. Perhaps the killer had thought he'd gotten away with the murder until I'd started poking around. The way the local grapevine worked in Danger Cove, I wouldn't be terribly surprised if Frank Dreiser had heard that I'd convinced Tony to talk to the police about Miriam's arguments with her ex-boss. If those arguments had led to Dreiser murdering Miriam, then he might well have decided to silence Tony before he could say anything to the police.

I squeezed Tony's hand, hoping he could feel it, despite his unconsciousness. "It's going to be okay."

I wasn't sure if that was true, and I felt as if what had happened to him was my fault. Not legally, of course. Only the person who'd attacked Tony could be charged with any wrongdoing. Still, I couldn't help thinking that I'd started the whole chain of events that led to Tony bleeding in Miriam's yard. If I'd stuck to my official job, appraising the quilts and not asking any questions about the murder, Tony might not have been targeted.

I couldn't do anything about his injuries, but I would do everything possible to make sure his attacker—and presumably also Miriam's killer—was brought to justice.

* * *

Officer Fred Fields was among the first to arrive in response to my 9-1-1 call. His expression was so grim, I wouldn't have been surprised if after the scene was cleared, he headed straight for the Cinnamon Sugar Bakery to eat his way through the entire menu.

"I don't like it," he said. "This is a nice neighborhood. Or it always used to be. And now, not just one, but two people were assaulted in a period of just a month."

"I'm not a professional like you," I said, "but I can't help believing the two incidents are related."

He glanced over his shoulder at where Detective Bud Ohlsen's vehicle had just arrived.

Fred leaned toward me to speak in a low tone. "I don't know what Bud's thinking—he doesn't like to commit to a theory before he's done some serious investigating—but I agree that both crimes have to be related. What really worries me is that the violence is escalating, in terms of intent. It's possible that Miriam's death could have been an accident, but all my years of experience tell me that what was done to Tony had to have been intentional, possibly even premeditated."

At the sound of Ohlsen's car door opening, Fred straightened and pulled out his official notebook. "Right. I need to take down a brief statement, along with the other witness's. Then you can both leave. The detective will contact you if he has any questions."

Once Fred was done with us, Craig gave me a ride to his office. There, I handed the notebook directly to Aaron and told him about the spreadsheets in the back and the attack on Tony Flores. Still in shock and acting on autopilot, I arranged to meet Craig at Miriam's the next morning to finish the inventory and then headed across the street to let Gil know the latest development.

I was approaching the stairs to the second floor of the museum when I heard my name being called. I turned to see Faith Miller with two preteens and a toddler—presumably her children—in the room dedicated to the lighthouse and its keepers. I went over to join them.

Faith sent the older children off to find three examples of the application of math to everyday life in the 1800s and picked up the toddler, propping him on her hip before she turned to me. "What can you tell me about what happened to Tony?"

I must have looked confused, because she continued. "Tony Flores, I mean. His cousin and I have been friends since we were born on the same day in the same hospital. I was on my way here when Sheila called. She wanted me to watch her kids when they get home from school this afternoon. At first, I was as happy as the kids were to have an excuse to abandon the math problems we'd been working on all morning. It's not my best subject—I always need to get help from the other quilters when I'm figuring out how much fabric I need for a new design—so it's hardly surprising that my kids struggle with numbers too. But then she told me that she was on the way to the hospital because Tony was injured and that you'd found him."

Faith's expression was tight, and I thought she was only holding herself together for her kids, not wanting to scare them. It had been hard enough to imagine her losing her temper with Miriam, but I really couldn't believe she'd have hurt Tony. She obviously cared about him and his cousin. Besides, I couldn't see how she could have nipped over to Miriam's house and attacked him while simultaneously homeschooling her children. If I was right that the two incidents were related, then Faith's alibi for Tony's attack meant that she also hadn't killed Miriam over the theft of her quilt design.

"I don't have any idea what happened after the ambulance took Tony away," I said. "I've been tied up with the police and then with Miriam's lawyer. I'm heading to the hospital to check on him right after I have a quick word with Gil."

"I won't keep you then," Faith said. "Would you let me know if you find out anything?"

"Of course." I glanced at the preteens, who were remarkably well-behaved, going from case to case, bickering only a little over the possible answers to their assignment. "I don't suppose you know anyone who might have wanted to hurt Tony, do you?"

"I don't know him well, but Sheila just adores him. Tony is an only child who envied other people their siblings, so they kind of adopted each other. Tony got a sister and Sheila got to hang out with an older brother instead of her pesky younger sisters." Faith peered at me anxiously. "Don't the police have any idea of what happened to him?"

"They didn't say anything to me, but I'm assuming their first thought was the same as mine, that it was related to Miriam's death somehow."

"But she died almost a month ago," Faith said, looking genuinely puzzled. "Why would anyone attack Tony now?"

I didn't want to speculate publicly, so I just said, "People who resort to violence aren't always rational."

"True." The bickering of Faith's kids was escalating slightly. She adjusted the toddler on her hip and turned to give the preteens her Evil Mom Look. They quieted down, and she turned back to me. "I can't imagine who would have hurt either Tony or Miriam. I didn't know Miriam very well, since she didn't come to many of the regular guild meetings. I was pretty angry with her—still am, really—but killing her wouldn't have fixed what she did to me. All I really wanted was an apology and an admission that she'd copied my design. I'll never get that now."

The younger of the preteens gave the older one a halfhearted shove, sending him into one of the—fortunately—sound exhibit cases with a slight thunk. Faith excused herself and hurried over to usher them out of the museum.

It was just as well. I needed to talk to Gil and then go to the hospital to find out what price Tony was paying for my meddling in a murder investigation.

* * *

Someday, I told myself, I was going to ask Gil to teach me the blues song she'd been singing as I left her office after giving her the news about Tony Flores. They lyrics were about having "troubles so hard," something I could relate to a little too well at the moment.

I caught a cab to the hospital and found my way to the intensive care unit visitors' room. Someone had tried to make the place more cheerful with some fresh floral arrangements, but they weren't enough to compensate for the industrial flooring, dingy walls, and faded upholstery.

Matt was there already, having heard about the incident from a colleague monitoring the local police scanner. I took the seat beside him, nearest the entrance.

The only other people in the room were two women at the opposite end, near the door that led into the ICU itself. One was older, at least in her sixties, in jeans and a pink knit tunic. Despite her red, puffy eyes, I could see the resemblance to Tony, suggesting that she was his mother.

The second woman was younger, somewhere in her thirties, with mousy brown hair, in chinos and a navy sport shirt.

She patted the hand of the older woman and came over to sit on the other side of Matt. Her lanky build and washed-out appearance had nothing in common with Tony's stockier build or darker coloring, but she introduced herself as his cousin, Sheila Flores.

"I'm Keely Fairchild. How's he doing?"

She looked over her shoulder at the older woman and lowered her voice. "They won't let me in to see him, so I'm getting all my information from his mother, and she's pretty distraught. All I know is Tony was hit on the back of his head, and there's internal bleeding putting pressure on his brain. Apparently, the doctors have put him into a medical coma, and they aren't saying for how long or even if he'll ever come out of it."

"I'm so sorry." Not just because Tony's condition sounded so serious, but also because if he was hit from behind, it meant he probably hadn't seen his attacker and couldn't identify him for the police.

I tried not to let my despair show. Sheila and Tony's mother were the ones who truly had *troubles so hard*, and I didn't want to distress them any further. "I've heard that the doctors here are amazing."

Sheila nodded. "I just can't understand any of this. Everyone loves Tony. My kids adore him. I sometimes think they're actually glad when I have to work overtime on the days when we've planned to go to Two Mile Beach, because it means Tony will take them there for me. And I've never heard anyone say anything negative about him. Why would anyone do this?"

"I was wondering that too," I said. "I've only known him a few days, but I can't picture him getting involved in any sort of a fight, physical or verbal."

"Oh, he'd get into fights." She smiled sadly. "Not brawls, but he wouldn't hesitate to get between a bully and his victim. In fact, he came home with a black eye a few weeks ago."

"Do you know who hit him?"

Sheila stared down at her hands for a moment before shaking her head. "He didn't mention any names. Just said someone was bothering a woman on his route, so he stepped in to try to calm things down. He can usually do that with just his goofy sense of humor. But not that time. The guy clocked him for interfering. Do you think that bully might have done this?"

"I know the detective on the case," I said. "I'll have a word with him. He may want to talk to you about that previous incident."

"I'll do anything that would help catch this person. It's just so unfair. Tony shouldn't even have been on that street today when he was attacked. He's usually done there by noon and home by 2:00 when my kids get out of school. So what was he doing still on his route at 3:00?" Sheila was distracted by a muffled sob from the older woman at the other end of the room. "I've got to go back to Aunt Josefina now. I'll try to remember more about how Tony got his black eye, though. Tell the detective he can find me at work at the Ocean View B&B most days."

"I will."

Sheila left, and Matt beckoned me out into the hallway, where we wouldn't be intruding on the privacy of Tony's family.

Once the door had shut behind us, Matt said, "I found Miriam's car."

He didn't go on to explain, so I prompted, "Well?"

He sighed. "I was hoping you'd throw yourself at me in gratitude and tell me what a brilliant reporter I am."

I raised my eyebrows. "I imagine you've had that happen with other women, but seriously? You expected that of *me*?"

"Not really," Matt said. "I like to be thorough though, so I had to see if you were at all susceptible to bribes."

"I'm not," I said. "And we're supposed to be in this together. You for your newspaper story and me for protecting the museum from bad publicity. Although I think that ship may have sailed. This is completely off the record, but I found evidence that Miriam had embezzled from her ex-boss, Frank Dreiser. He was seen at her house a few days before she died, so I'm wondering if he finally noticed her embezzlement when he was preparing for the sale of his business assets and went to confront her about it. That would make him the prime suspect, as far as I'm concerned."

"Then you don't think her missing car has anything to do with her murder? And you don't want to know where her car is?"

Matt looked so disappointed, I would have let him tell me what he'd found out, even if I weren't curious. "I'm not certain about Dreiser. Just inclined to believe it was him unless you can tell me something particularly interesting about Miriam's car."

"I'm not sure how interesting it is, but her car is at a repair shop," he said. "She dropped it off a few days before she died, and they must have missed the news about her death, because they've been wondering why she hadn't come to pick it up. They're a little anxious about getting paid for their repairs."

"I'll let Aaron Pohoke know," I said. "Did they tell you what was wrong with the car?"

"Pretty much everything, according to the mechanic," Matt said. "And he wasn't just saying that to sell some unnecessary work to a clueless customer. He showed me the intake sheet, and there was a note that Miriam had told them she'd been sold a lemon and the car had been worked on by the dealership where she bought it practically once a week since she bought it. She'd finally gotten fed up and taken it to this place to find out what was really wrong with it. They thought the car had been in a major accident, perhaps declared a total loss, and then someone had done the very minimum of repairs before selling it to Miriam."

"I met Wayne Good, the guy who sold the car to Miriam, and he's probably right behind Dreiser as a prime suspect in her death," I said. "I got the impression that he'd been pretending to be her friend, first to sell her the car, and then later to keep her from returning it as a lemon. I couldn't picture him in a real relationship with Miriam. He was outright dismissive of the only thing she seemed to care about—her quilts—when he was talking to me."

"That makes him sound like a jerk, but not necessarily a killer."

"There's more," I said. "He was a little too anxious to get inside Miriam's house, and I can't help thinking that he knew about the cash hidden there and was hoping to grab it. I'd give a lot to know if Wayne had found out that Miriam wasn't blinded by him any longer and had had the car taken to the garage."

"You think that if Wayne knew Miriam was on to him, he might have gone to her house to try to smooth things over, and instead they got into an argument, and he killed her?"

"I think it's possible."

"While you finish up the quilt inventory, I'll see if I can find out more about this Wayne Good and where he was on the day Miriam was killed," Matt said. "Unless there's something else I can do to help you finish the work at Miriam's house so we can set a date to tour your bank vault?"

I couldn't help thinking of poor Miriam, and how she'd trusted Wayne Good, inviting him into her home and her heart. It was likely she'd been taken advantage of, and possibly even been killed, because of her failure to anticipate what could go wrong with their relationship.

But I wasn't Miriam, and Matt wasn't Wayne.

The worst that could happen when Matt saw the contents of my vault was that his image of me would be shattered, and he wouldn't like the real me. Putting it off would only delay the inevitable.

"We can set the date for the bank vault tour now," I said, apparently taking him by surprise. "I'm guessing it'll take you an hour or two to check out Wayne's alibi. I can't go back to Miriam's house until tomorrow, but I would like to talk to someone about the quilt guild's meeting space before I go home. It shouldn't take long, though. Why don't you stop by my place whenever you've got some information on Wayne?"

Matt glanced at his watch. "I've got a meeting at the newspaper at 4:00. I'll come by after that. I can pick up something for dinner on the way."

CHAPTER SEVENTEEN

I was certain Jack Condor wouldn't change his mind about evicting the guild, and I doubted he'd even consider letting them use another building he owned, but he wasn't the only person in his office who might know about available space. Despite Bonnie's seemingly low status as the receptionist, she probably knew more about the company's real estate holdings than Condor did.

I caught a cab to the outskirts of town and found Bonnie at her desk, staring in the direction of the corridor that led to the conference room. She didn't even seem to notice my arrival until I closed the door behind me.

Bonnie started guiltily and then smiled at me in relief. "For a second there, I thought the boss had come back early. He hates it when I don't look busy. He doesn't care if I'm *actually* busy, as long as I look impressive for any visitors."

"I try to look beyond appearances," I said. "That's why I'm here, in fact. I think you have more say in what goes on here than Jack Condor would admit. He said there wasn't anywhere else for the quilt guild to meet in any of his properties, but I was hoping you'd know of a place he might have overlooked."

She pursed her artificially full lips and shook her head. "I wish I did. I tried to come up with something when Jack first told me he was planning to evict the guild, but there's nothing available right now. Everything is either rented out, in the midst of renovations, or in such bad shape that it wouldn't be safe for anyone to use the property."

"What about the assets he's buying from Frank Dreiser?"

"I haven't had a chance to look them over yet," Bonnie said. "You probably noticed that Dreiser doesn't trust women. He won't let me into the conference room, as if I wouldn't see everything eventually."

I could hear the rumble of a male voice talking in the conference room. Condor wasn't here, and I doubted the shy teen who worked here would be that loud. Adding in the way that Bonnie had been staring in that direction, I suspected the voice belonged to Dreiser. I needed to talk to him, and then I might be able to figure out if he was the one who'd given Tony a black eye a few weeks back. If so, that would definitely make him the prime suspect in Tony's attack and possibly also Miriam's death, ahead of Wayne Good and Herb Stafford.

"Is Dreiser here now?"

Bonnie hesitated, although the flicker of a glance toward the conference room answered my question. "He was pretty angry with you the last time you were here."

"I hope he didn't take it out on you."

She shook her head. "He pretty much ignores me because of his 'all women are cheating, lying thieves' theory."

If anyone was a cheating, lying thief, I thought, Dreiser was.

I didn't think we could be heard as far away as the conference room, but just in case, I leaned over Bonnie's desk and lowered my voice. "Keep an eye on him. He's already thinking about ignoring the non-compete agreement with your boss."

"I'm not surprised. But thanks for the heads-up." Bonnie jerked open the bottom drawer of her desk and pulled out her bag. "I'm sorry I can't stay and chat, but I really need to take my afternoon coffee break right now. I'll be gone for exactly fifteen minutes, and Jack isn't due back for hours, if he comes back at all today."

"Thanks."

I waited until the outer door shut behind her so she had plausible deniability. I didn't bother knocking on the conference room door, just let myself in.

"I told you—" Dreiser began as he turned around. "Oh. It's you. I thought it was that bimbo from the front desk. Change your mind about letting me take a look inside Miriam's house? I'm still willing to make it worth your while."

He couldn't possibly make it worth my while, but I was here to get information from him, not antagonize him. "The only thing I could use right now is a new meeting place for the quilt guild, but you've signed away all your properties."

Dreiser glanced over his shoulder at the teen behind the laptop before winking at me. "Yeah, that was the deal. But I'm wily. And I know people. If I can't find something myself, I might be able to generate some leads for you."

Only my long years of experience as a lawyer dealing with bad-faith negotiators kept me from rolling my eyes. I could bend the truth as well as he could. "I have leads. What I don't have is a good reason to explain why I let you inside Miriam's house if anyone notices. It would be different if I knew you were a close friend of hers, but I heard that you created a scene the last time you visited her."

He raised his hands in the classic gesture of innocence. "That wasn't my fault. It was that interfering little busybody who started it."

"What busybody was that?"

"The mail carrier," he said. "He shouldn't have gotten involved in something that was none of his business."

"If you were arguing with Miriam, he might have been concerned for her."

Dreiser snorted. "Miriam could take care of herself. She certainly did while she worked for me. Covered her tracks really well too. I only found out what she'd done when I was going over some records as part of this deal with Condor. She was a lying, cheating thief. Worse than most women. Claimed she was an excellent bookkeeper always looking out for my interests, when the only thing she was good at was lining her own pockets."

So Dreiser did know about the embezzlement. And so would Detective Ohlsen, once Aaron Pohoke gave him Miriam's journal. I was confident that Dreiser was soon going to be on the very top of their suspect list.

I didn't want to tip him off, so I pretended not to know what he meant about Miriam's stealing from him. "If you were mad at Miriam, then I can see why Tony might have been concerned about her safety."

"He's as bad as she was," Dreiser said. "Stupid, lying little jerk. You know, he even went and told the cops today that I probably killed Miriam. Good thing I have some friends on the force, and they watch out for me, or I wouldn't even know he was telling tales about me."

It was news to me that Tony had already been to the police station, but whether it was true or not, Dreiser believed it, so he had a reason to try to silence a potential witness against him. A written statement by Tony, while potentially admissible at trial, wasn't as convincing as a live witness.

"Why would Tony blame you for Miriam's death?"

"Could have been payback for the black eye I gave him, but I think it was to throw the detectives off his own scent. He had a cozy little arrangement with Miriam. Probably stealing her blind bit by bit under cover of making package deliveries." Dreiser shook his head with false regret. "I guess it's too bad I didn't press charges against the little jerk back then, but I thought I was being the better man, letting it go. I could have gotten him fired from the post office, and perhaps the police would have figured out that he was taking advantage of Miriam before he killed her."

"Press charges for what?" I asked. "He was the one with a black eye."

"He started it." Dreiser smirked. "He only got what he deserved."

"Did he deserve what happened to him today too?"

"How the heck should I know what happened to him today? Whatever it was, it's got nothing to do with me. I've been stuck in this room for yet another whole day, finishing up the paperwork, because this kid—" He jerked his thumb in the direction of the redheaded teen at the laptop. "—is the best that Condor could spare. I suppose I should be grateful I don't have to work with that airhead from the front desk."

I wouldn't take Dreiser's word for whether it was sunny outside, so I certainly wasn't going to take his word for where he'd been when Tony was attacked.

I looked at the teen. "Have you both been here all day? Neither of you left the building since you got here this morning?"

The kid nodded, apparently still too nervous to speak.

"I don't have time for this," Dreiser snapped. "I've got a plane reservation for Monday, and I have a lot to wrap up before then."

I wasn't going to get any further information from him, so I left him to his work. At least I knew that he had an alibi for the assault on Tony. That also made it considerably less likely that he'd killed Miriam. Still, I wasn't ready to cross him off the suspect list quite yet.

What worried me most was that if he had killed Miriam and it took too long to find the evidence against him, he might get away with it. While he might theoretically be extradited, practical considerations like the cost of the legal process meant that it was likely that once Dreiser made it to Mexico then for all intents and purposes, he'd be out of the reach of the Danger Cove Police Department.

* * *

I got home with about half an hour to spare before Matt was due to arrive. As I tidied up the bank vault, I had some second thoughts—or, more accurately, two-hundredth thoughts—about whether I was ready to let Matt see the real me, as reflected in the contents of the vault.

I never would have considered it back when I first met Matt, but I'd come to learn that he was very different from my first impression of him as a brainless pretty boy. In fact, if it hadn't been for his insights into a previous murder investigation, I might have been killed shortly after I'd moved to Danger Cove. At the time, especially when he'd subsequently disappeared for months without a word, I'd thought he'd only been using me to get a scoop on the story, but he'd come through for me again when I needed his help a few months ago to solve a murder at the museum.

As I fluffed the pillows in the overstuffed chairs inside the vault, I decided I was being unfair to Matt again, expecting the worst from him. I'd never been any good at letting people get too close to me, starting when I was a child. As an adult, my legal training had made it doubly difficult to trust anyone, even with something as relatively innocuous as seeing the contents of my vault. A trained observer, like a journalist, could tell a lot from the contents of the private spaces in a home.

Surprisingly, my stomach wasn't churning, and there were no signs of incipient lightheadedness. I found that reassuring, although perhaps I'd tricked my nervous system with wishful thinking about how Matt might react to the contents of the vault.

Before I could work myself up into a bundle of nerves, I heard Matt knocking. When I opened the outer door to the converted ATM lobby, he was waiting for me with the expected pizza carton, but it was topped with an unexpected bouquet of spring flowers in a box that looked like an inverted Chinese take-out container, except that it was dark green and featured the logo of Some Enchanted Florist.

I let Matt in, and he carried everything over to the peninsula that separated the kitchen from the living room.

I'd never felt quite so awkward around Matt before, but we'd always been too busy with quilt-related events or a murder investigation for me to worry much about my image. Now, all I could think of was the way more than a few colleagues in the past had reacted with disdain and derision toward the things I enjoyed outside of work. Quiltmaking wasn't the only activity that people—especially male people—considered a foolish waste of time.

I grabbed the florist box and took it over to the sink. "It would be a shame to let such beautiful flowers wilt."

"Is that a stalling tactic?"

I tended to forget how good Matt's instincts were. He must have picked up on my tension.

"I'm just being practical." I ran the water until it was room temperature. "I want these flowers to last as long as possible. George Fontaine's bouquets are works of art. Did you know that even the previous owner of the shop was in awe of his design skills?"

Matt didn't answer, and I realized I was babbling. If my ex-colleagues could hear me now, they'd wonder how I'd managed to get through a motion session, let alone a whole trial, without ranting incoherently.

This was different though. I'd always been better at presenting other people's cases than my own. Plus, none of the opposing counsel had ever brought me flowers from Some Enchanted Florist.

"Look," Matt said, "if you're not ready to do this, that's okay. I'm a patient person."

I'd faced down skeptical juries in multi-million dollar cases. I could handle whatever Matt's reaction was to the vault. I took a deep breath, drew myself up and turned around to face him. "No, it's fine. I did promise."

"You make it sound like you're steeling yourself to do something painful," Matt said. "Like tearing off a bandage. I'm guessing you like to do it fast and get the pain over with quickly. Me, I prefer to go slowly, in the hope of avoiding the pain completely. But we can do it however you choose. Shall we tour the vault before dinner or after?"

Normally, he was right about my jerking the bandage off as fast as possible. I just wasn't prepared for the possible pain yet.

"Let's eat first," I said finally.

Matt opened the pizza box. "I was hoping you'd say that. I'm starved. And I've got news."

I retrieved two plates and placed them on the peninsula. "First, do you want beer, wine, or water?"

"Beer would be good." He settled onto one of the stools and put a pizza slice on each plate. "Before the meeting at the newspaper, I dug up some information on Wayne Good. Did you know that's not his legal name? It's actually Hobgood, but he shortens it for work. Apparently thinks it makes potential buyers more receptive to his sales pitches. His co-workers weren't impressed by either his name or his skills. They told me he sees himself as the Wayne Gretzky of car sales, while everyone else sees him as Wayne from *Wayne's World*."

"I wonder if Miriam knew his real name." I handed him his beer and fetched a glass of water for myself. "She mentioned him in a list of people she was angry with, but she used his pseudonym."

"Wait," Matt said, holding his pizza slice in mid-air. "Miriam wrote her own list of suspects for killing her?"

I nodded. "A person after my own heart, taking precautions against all possible contingencies."

"Who else is on the list?"

"Dreiser. That was part of why he was my prime suspect, but then I talked to him this afternoon, and he has an alibi for when Tony was attacked. Assuming Miriam's killer is also the one who injured Tony too, then it can't be Dreiser."

"Are you sure the two events are related?"

"Not entirely, but it seems the most likely scenario." I took a bite of the pizza—excellent, as always—while I thought. "If Dreiser has an alibi, it puts Wayne at the top of the remaining suspects. Her neighbors, Dani and Lou Hudson, are another possibility. They needed Miriam's cooperation to clear up a title issue, so they could sell the house, and she wasn't cooperating. I haven't met the husband, but Dani said he's really anxious to move closer to his work, so perhaps he ran out of patience with their negotiations."

"I'll see if I can find anything out about him," Matt said. "Anyone else a suspect?"

"It's a real long shot, but there's a quilter who thinks Miriam stole her design. She talked to a lawyer about it but was told she didn't have a case worth pursuing. That sort of frustration over not having any legal redress can fester until a small slight gets completely blown out of proportion and the victim starts to act irrationally."

"Gotta watch out for those quilters," Matt said with a grin. "I definitely wouldn't turn my back on Emma if I'd ever wronged Dee."

"I can imagine Emma running someone out of town, but I don't think she'd ever assault anyone. Or smother anyone to death with a pile of quilts. If only because Emma wouldn't want to risk damaging the quilts."

"True." Matt finished his slice of pizza, lifted the box lid, and then let it fall, apparently deciding he was full. "There was something else I wanted to tell you. I ran into a colleague, Duncan Pickles, on the way to the meeting today, and I could tell he thought he had some big scoop. It's probably a good thing he doesn't really have any competition around here, because he can never sit on a story until it goes into print. He drops so many hints a competitor could do his own research and publish the piece before Duncan did."

"Is that what you're planning to do? Steal the guy's story?" I asked. "I thought you were a mild-mannered arts reporter who didn't care about scoops."

"I am. Besides, I'm pretty sure Duncan's story is false. He heard a rumor that someone at the museum had either killed Miriam or hired it done in order to expedite the inheritance."

"That's ludicrous." I pushed my plate back, no longer hungry. If Gil heard that rumor, she'd be searching for an even more depressing song than the last one I'd heard. The blues had always struck me as implying at least some degree of hope and an awareness that sharing the misery would lighten it a little. If Duncan's story got out, the blues might be too upbeat for Gil's mood.

"No one at the museum even knew about the bequest until after Miriam died," I said. "Even if someone had found out, they wouldn't have known about the cash we found. Even Miriam's attorney didn't know about it. She'd been hiding its existence for something like twenty years, so I doubt she'd started blabbing about it recently."

"Whoever killed Miriam probably started the rumor," Matt said. "Duncan would know that if he weren't so blinded by his desire for a scoop."

I'd once thought Matt was like that, only caring about his stories. Now, I knew there was a lot more to him. I abandoned the last of my pizza slice and stood.

"We aren't going to solve Miriam's murder without some more information," I said. "If you'll find out more about Dani's husband, I'll check on whether Wayne has an alibi for when Miriam was killed."

"Right now?" he asked plaintively and glanced in the direction of the bank vault.

"Not quite yet." I took his hand and led him out of the great room and into a hallway that led to the vault.

The massive vault door was open, affixed against the wall with heavy metal fixtures, its locking mechanism disabled as an extra precaution against anyone getting trapped inside. Inside were two over-sized, over-stuffed chairs and a small table with a reading light. Over the concrete floor, I'd had thick, wall-to-wall carpeting installed.

I waited in the hallway while Matt went inside. I concentrated on keeping my breaths deep and slow to control my anxiety.

Matt peered at what used to be safe deposit boxes lining all the walls. They'd been replaced with built-in floor-to-ceiling wood shelves.

He turned to me, his face radiating approval. "A reading room. That's perfect."

"I thought so," I said, still wary about his response would be once he started reading the titles on the spines.

He leaned in closer to do just that, and ran his index finger over a row of books in the mystery section. "It looks like you've got every single one of Elizabeth Ashby's books." He tugged one of them out. "Including my favorite, *Secret of the Painted Lady*." He flipped it open to the title page. "Signed, even."

If it was true, as author Geraldine Brooks wrote, that to know a person's library was to know her mind, Matt didn't seem at all put off by my mind. I'd apparently been worrying for nothing.

"I've been a fan of Elizabeth Ashby since her first book," I said. "That was back when I still lived in Seattle, so it wasn't easy getting them all signed. I had to drive down here to signings at Dangerous Reads."

Matt continued around the room, reading out an occasional title approvingly. Not surprisingly, he wasn't as familiar with the romance titles, but when he reached the fantasy area, the last one before he'd have completed the circuit of the room, he frowned.

I braced myself for the type of negative comments I'd gotten before, the ones pointing out the lack of any "serious" fiction and questioning why a smart, well-educated person would read nothing but popular fiction. I did have the collected works of Shakespeare, but that was about it for anything that might be considered literature with a capital L.

Matt reached the very end of the shelves and faced me. "Where's the science fiction? That's my favorite genre."

I finally let myself relax and entered the vault with a light step. "I don't read a lot of science fiction, so I include them in the fantasy section." I pointed to a handful of books he must have missed. "See? Bujold's Vorkosigan series, and Ann Leckie's *Imperial Radch* series."

"I keep meaning to read the Vorkosigan books. Which one should I start with?"

I handed him my well-worn copy of *Shards of Honor*, and he carried it over to one of the reading chairs. He dropped into the seat and began reading out loud. I'd never followed his previous career, but now I could understand more about why he'd been such an internet sensation. His reading voice was as appealing as his face.

After about a page, he looked up. "Well? What do you think? The acoustics in here are pretty amazing."

Nowhere near as amazing as Matt himself was. "I think you should keep reading."

"Only if you'll come sit with me. Every performer needs an audience."

I started past him, but he lightly snagged my wrist and pulled me down to share his chair. I settled my back against his chest while he reached around me to hold the book with two hands.

As he continued to read, I was aware of the masculine scent of him and the even beat of his heart. I could hear the rumble of his voice and the occasional turn of the page, but I couldn't concentrate on the actual words. My pulse sped up, and I was definitely tense, and it struck me that I hadn't been in a romantic relationship since my syncope diagnosis. Would I pass out if Matt paused in his reading to kiss me?

Sometimes the best way to deal with anxiety was to confront the issue head on, like the bandage-ripping scenario we'd discussed earlier. All I had to do was turn a bit in Matt's arms, and I could kiss him and see whether the earth would move or I would pass out and miss all the fun.

CHAPTER EIGHTEEN

———

I didn't get the chance to find out what would happen if I kissed Matt.

Before I could turn, we were interrupted by honking out in the parking lot insistent enough that even the thick walls and carpeting of the vault couldn't muffle it. I did consider for a moment whether I'd made a mistake in making sure the heavy metal door couldn't be shut, but by then Matt had stopped reading aloud and set aside the book, preparing to stand.

I got to my feet and jogged out to the great room where I could see who was causing the ruckus.

Dee and Emma were getting out of their car. My little bit of medical research would have to wait for another day.

As I let the women inside, Dee said, "We saw Matt's truck outside, so we knew you were home. We decided to stop in and see if you've convinced Jack Condor to do the right thing yet. We're running out of time to let our members know where our future meetings will be."

"I've been a little busy."

"I suppose a murder investigation can be time-consuming," Dee conceded.

"We also wanted to know if there was any news about Tony Flores," Emma added. "We didn't get a chance to ask you earlier. Is he going to be okay?"

I looked to Matt, in case he had an update.

"I haven't heard anything since Keely and I left the hospital earlier today," he said. "I'd have heard from one of my colleagues if he'd taken a turn for the worse, so he must be stable."

"Tony's a good person," Dee said as she settled in a chair in the great room. "He helped Miriam set up a special exhibit dedicated to cheddar quilts at the annual show a few years ago. He spent an entire day with her, sorting out which quilts to include in the display and then transporting them to the show's site."

"That was kind of him," I said, even as I was wondering if, as Dreiser had suggested, Tony had been motivated by something other than the goodness of his heart. Being suspicious was part of both my nature and my legal training.

Tony definitely interacted with his postal patrons more than the average mail carrier. Or at least with Miriam. I hated to even think it, but perhaps Frank Dreiser wasn't completely wrong that Tony might have had designs on Miriam's assets. It wasn't unheard of for greedy people to worm their way into an isolated, unhealthy person's life as a long-term investment in benefitting from the person's will someday, occasionally even going so far as to kill in order to speed up the inheritance. I'd never heard of a mail carrier doing anything like that before—usually it was an extended family member or some service provider accused of that kind of behavior—but a postal route would definitely serve up a large number of potential victims.

Even as naturally suspicious as I was, I had a hard time reconciling that kind of calculated behavior with Tony. Besides, in order to believe he'd been the one to attack Miriam, I'd also have to believe that he'd attacked himself today to remove himself from suspicion in Miriam's death. I couldn't see how he could have accomplished that. Of course, he might have had an accomplice, so I couldn't rule out the possibility completely.

"I'll let you know if I hear anything more about Tony's condition," I promised.

"Me too," Matt said.

"Good," Dee said. "Then all we have to worry about is the guild meeting space. It looks like we'll have to pull out the big guns."

I was reasonably certain—but there was some room for doubt—that she was speaking metaphorically. "Do I want to know what you've got planned?"

"It's okay," Emma said from her spot at Dee's shoulder. "We're just going to picket Jack Condor's office building until he does right by us."

Condor wouldn't hesitate to have the entire guild arrested if he could come up with grounds to do it. And if the woman-hating, assault-provoking Frank Dreiser was there too, things could get really ugly.

"Just give me until the end of Monday before you do anything at Condor's office," I said. "I'm almost done with the work on Miriam's inventory, and once that's finished I'll be able to spend more time on finding new space for you."

Dee grumbled a bit under her breath, but she didn't resist Emma's efforts to escort her out to their car. Matt followed in their wake, explaining that he had a deadline, but he'd get back to me with what he learned about Dani's husband as a possible suspect in Miriam's death.

I didn't try to keep him from leaving. The mood was broken, and I had deadlines of my own. Too many of them for the stress-free life I was supposed to be living. I thought I'd left most of the pressing time constraints behind me when I quit practicing law, but instead I'd just moved laterally, accumulating new deadlines. Now, instead of worrying about the court's schedule, I was fretting over the quilt guild's relocation, Gil's telling the board of directors about Miriam's embezzlement, and what looked to be the very real possibility that Tony's attacker and Miriam's killer might never be arrested.

* * *

After everyone left, I checked the hours for the nearby town's car dealership where Wayne Good worked. I had another hour before they closed, so I decided to go see if he was there.

As I climbed out of the cab, a swarm of sales reps headed in my direction. Wayne was toward the back, checking something on his phone. When he looked up and caught sight of me, he pushed his way to the front.

"She's mine," he told his colleagues. "I know her, and she's a woman of discerning taste in cars." With a smarmy smile, he added, "And in men."

Wayne was right about my taste in men, just not about how I rated him.

Still, I let him separate me from the other salesmen. "I'm not here to buy a car. I just thought you'd want to know that Miriam's car has been found."

"Are you sure you aren't in the market for a car?" He was clearly aiming for winsome, but his tone and facial expression just irritated me. "I could really use the sale for this month's quota. I've been here since we opened this morning, making calls and showing vehicles without a single break."

If that was true, then he couldn't have attacked Tony.

I glanced past Wayne at the other sales reps who were sending metaphorical daggers at their colleague and whispering among themselves. They seemed truly hostile toward Wayne, something more than might be expected among colleagues who competed for commissions. They wouldn't be inclined to lie for Wayne if asked about his alibi. I'd have to come back later and ask them when Wayne wasn't here.

"It sounds like you've had a long day," I said. "Did you meet your quota?"

He shook his head. "Not yet, but I will. We just got in a sweet little Miata. Someone's going to snap it up, and it could be you. You'd look amazing behind the wheel of a ride like that."

Not if I passed out and then rammed the car into a tree and my face into the airbag.

I wasn't about to tell Wayne that was the reason why I preferred not to drive a car. I didn't even trust Matt with that information, although after the experience in the vault, I might be willing to share considerably more than just my reading room with him.

"I'm happy without a car," I said, which was mostly true. "I can walk most places in Danger Cove, and I don't need the hassle of maintaining a car. Taking it in for oil changes and all. That's where Miriam's car was, by the way. She left it at a repair shop shortly before she died."

"Why didn't she just bring it here?" Wayne oozed what was supposed to come across as concern for Miriam, but I caught a glimpse of irritation in his eyes. "We'd have fixed any tiny problem she might have had with it. I take care of all my customers."

Especially the vulnerable ones like Miriam.

"So you didn't know she'd taken it to the competition?"

He blinked, and this time his emotion—surprise—did appear genuine. "Why would I know something like that?"

Oftentimes answering a question with a question was a sure sign of a lie, but I didn't think so in this case. I couldn't be sure unless I pushed him a little harder. "You were close enough to have had your personal effects inside Miriam's house. I would have thought you'd notice if her car wasn't in the driveway when you visited and then asked about it."

"Our relationship wasn't what you think." Wayne waved a dismissive hand, as if he hadn't been the one to make it sound like he'd been close to Miriam. "Nothing truly intimate. I just left my reading glasses there. Miriam liked it when I read to her while she worked on her quilts."

Wayne did have a nice voice. Probably thanks to a voice tutor, I thought suspiciously. Too bad he hadn't found an equally good instructor for his people skills.

"Still, since you sold her the car, I would have thought you'd be the first to hear that she thought it was a lemon."

"That's a lie," he said. "All of our cars are first-rate. Some people just don't know how to drive properly. Miriam hadn't owned a car in ten or fifteen years, so she didn't know what modern cars are like. She couldn't understand that there was nothing wrong with hers."

"The mechanic at the other shop had a long list of critical repairs that the car needed."

Wayne shook his head. "Just another bad mechanic trying to cheat a customer. There was absolutely nothing wrong with that car. I checked it out myself."

"When was that?"

He shrugged. "About a week before she died. I thought she'd accepted the truth finally. I was pretty busy between then and her death, though, so I didn't have time to visit her. It was the last week of the month, just like now, and it's always crazy when we get down to the wire on the monthly quota."

"You must have been working the day Miriam died, then."

He nodded. "I wish I'd had time to visit her. Maybe I could have saved her."

"Or the killer could have gotten you too," I said.

"I can handle myself." Wayne demonstrated by assuming a boxer's pose, clenching his fists and throwing a few jabs at the air.

His right hand seemed red and slightly swollen. From punching someone? Tony, perhaps, before hitting him on the head? That seemed unlikely. I didn't really believe that Wayne was much of a pugilist, and Tony was strong and fit, carrying that huge mailbag and walking his route. Of course, it didn't take a lot of skill to bash someone on the head.

Wayne dropped his fighting pose. "I wouldn't even need a fraction of my skills to take on Miriam's killer. Herb Stafford is a weasel."

Was he just trying to implicate someone else, or did he know something that I didn't? "Why do you think Miriam's cousin killed her?"

"I didn't in the beginning," he said. "At first, I thought it was her neighbors. They're really desperate to sell their house, and they needed Miriam's cooperation with clearing the title. I tried to help with the deal, but the Hudsons were completely unreasonable in their demands."

"And yet, you changed your mind about suspecting them?"

"Yeah," Wayne said. "The Hudsons are going to have an even worse time dealing with the estate's attorney than with me, so killing Miriam wouldn't make things better for them. I mean, I'm skilled at putting together deals, and lawyers—no disrespect intended—are usually better at ruining deals than making them happen. So that leaves Miriam's cousin as the only person who might have wanted her dead. He was her only relative, so he had to know he was likely to come into a good bit of money when she died, and she certainly wasn't going to share any of it with him when she was alive. The last time I visited her Herb was there, and they were arguing over money again. He wanted a loan, but Miriam knew she'd never get a penny of it back. She told him that just because they were cousins didn't give him any claim on her money. No one had given her anything she hadn't earned, so it was up to him to get his own money, just like she'd done. He complained that she was hard-hearted, and she told him that if he didn't like the way she felt, that was his problem, and he should just go away and leave her alone. Permanently."

"That does sound a bit cold," I said. "She could have turned him down without getting quite so harsh about it."

"That's just how Miriam was. Didn't have the best people skills. She'd never have been able to sell her quilts in person. Doing it online, she didn't have to haggle or anything." He shrugged. "Not everyone can be as good at sales as I am. Besides, I don't think Herb would have accepted a nicer brush-off."

"I've met a few people like that." Like Wayne himself.

He looked over his shoulder at the other sales reps who'd been watching us all along. Turning back to me, he said, "So, are you sure you wouldn't like to take a test ride in the Miata? Or perhaps something bigger and more rugged. You don't need a chick car. You could handle something with more power."

"Thanks, but I've got all the power I'm interested in."

CHAPTER NINETEEN

———

The next morning, I walked more briskly than normal on the way to Miriam's, anxious to get the work finished, and when I reached her street, there was no sign of Craig's truck. I was a little early—another habit left over from my days as a trial lawyer—so I wasn't concerned. I slowed my pace to give him time to arrive. After everything that had happened, I wasn't foolish enough to go near the house without him.

Dani Hudson must have been watching for me, because as soon as I was within sight of her front windows, she came jogging into the yard, wearing yet another massively oversized muumuu, this one in a red and black batik. "Have you heard how Tony's doing? I called the hospital and his boss at the post office, but they won't tell me anything."

"His cousin told me he had some swelling in his brain, so they put him in a medical coma," I said, "but that was yesterday afternoon. I don't have any updates since then."

"Poor Tony. I wonder what he was doing when he was attacked. Normally, I'd have said he was helping someone, but it was too late to help Miriam." Dani nodded at Craig's truck coming down the street. "And you already had a bodyguard."

"I was hoping you might have seen something that would help the police find his attacker."

She shook her head. "I wouldn't have been able to see anything. From what I saw of the police search afterwards, it happened in the blind spot where I can't see the yard from my house. Besides, I wasn't home at the time. I was at our lawyer's office. It looks like we can finally get our title problem straightened out and sell the house now. My husband will be so relieved when I tell him."

"He's still out of town?"

"For a few more days," Dani said. "I'm waiting until he gets back before I share the news. I don't want to get his hopes up about selling the house until I'm absolutely sure it's going to happen. We've celebrated too many times already when we thought we had the problem resolved only to have the deal fall apart."

A month was a long time for a business trip, and I only had Dani's word for her husband's whereabouts. Another possible explanation was that he had killed Miriam and then left town where he'd have a head start on disappearing if anyone began to suspect him of the murder. I hoped Matt could figure out where Lou Hudson was. The neighbors definitely had a motive, since it looked like they would finally be able to sell their house now that Miriam was dead.

The only problem with that theory was that it conflicted with my belief that the assault on Tony was related to Miriam's death. I supposed it was possible that in the course of talking to the police, Tony had recalled something that might implicate the Hudsons, and that was why he'd been attacked. But if Lou had been out of town all this time, as Dani claimed, he couldn't have been the attacker yesterday. Could Dani have attacked Tony? She was small, but it didn't take that much strength or skill to bash someone on the head. On the other hand, she claimed to have been with her attorney when the attack happened. Whether or not it was true, it was a difficult alibi for the police to shake since the attorney couldn't ethically dispute her statement without a court order.

The slamming of Craig's truck door reminded me that I needed to get to work if I wanted to finish the inventory before anything else could go wrong.

"I've got to go," I said. "But I'll let you know if I have any news about Tony's condition."

"Thanks," Dani said. "I hope they catch whoever did it. I just wish I'd been here and had seen him leaving. Then I could have identified him for the police. As it is, all we've got is speculation. I've talked to all the neighbors, and most of them think it was that Dreiser person. They had words a few weeks ago, you know. But I hadn't seen him here since then, so I'm not sure he's guilty. It's easy to blame Dreiser though, since no one likes him. He's come nosing around the neighborhood a few times, trying to get people to sell him their homes."

"That's his job, nothing personal."

"Not the way he does it," Dani said. "Once he lied about some environmental contamination, and then when a housing bubble burst a few years ago, he told everyone their houses were going to be totally worthless in another six months, so he'd be doing them a favor by paying them half of the market value. He got nasty when people turned him down."

"Did he assault anyone?"

"No. Mostly Dreiser just riled up other people." She frowned thoughtfully. "Although he did throw things when he was angry. Anything he could get his hands on. Maybe that's what happened to Tony. Dreiser threw something in a fit of pique, and it just happened to hit Tony's head. And Dreiser could have killed Miriam too by throwing the quilts while he was having a tantrum. He might not even have realized they landed on top of her."

"You don't sound entirely convinced that Dreiser's guilty."

"I'm not. For one thing, I saw Miriam arguing with Dreiser the day Tony intervened, and I don't think she'd have let him in her house after that. He couldn't have thrown the quilts at her from the front porch. For another, even if she did let him inside, I don't think she'd have been relaxed enough to sit in her recliner. She didn't really use the living room the way most people did. She thought of it as a working room for her quilts, and she didn't like people messing with anything in there. She brought visitors into the kitchen to sit at the dining table. She only sat in her recliner when she was doing some hand stitching."

"So how did the killer catch her in the living room?"

"It had to have been someone she knew," Dani said. "She left the front door unlocked whenever she was expecting a visitor. Otherwise, she'd get breathless in the rush to answer the door."

"She wouldn't do that for relative strangers, I imagine."

"Oh, no," Dani said. "I can only think of a few people she trusted at all. She used to leave it open for me until recently, when our negotiations fell apart. She used to do it for her cousin too, but not in the last year or so. Not since she lost her patience with his frequent requests for loans. Mostly, the only person I know that she left it unlocked for was Wayne. That's why he's my number-one suspect in her death."

"No one else she might have left the door unlocked for?"

"No one who had any reason to hurt her," Dani said. "She hired a number of different contractors from time to time, but from what they told me, she paid in cash and never quibbled about a bill. She was the kind of customer small businesses only dream of."

"Did she have any work done shortly before she died?"

Dani tugged at the excess fabric of her dress while she thought and briefly looked down at her lawn, still somewhat patchy from the winter. "You know, I'd forgotten about it, but she'd just had a spring clean-up done on her yard. I always thought it was a little surprising that she took such good care of the property, since she hardly ever spent any time outside, but she did make sure the yard was well maintained and mowed regularly."

I looked over at Miriam's home, and the grass was a little shaggy from three weeks of being untouched, but it was much neater than it would have been without proper maintenance before she'd died.

I also noticed that Craig had gone over to the porch to wait for me, but instead of sitting there as relaxed as he'd been other times, he was pacing restlessly. He probably had better things to do on a Saturday than to babysit me. Unfortunately, I couldn't release him from his duties here. After yesterday, it really wasn't safe for me to be at Miriam's house alone. I was beginning to worry that it wasn't even safe for the tough-looking Craig. The sooner I finished the inventory, the better it would be for everyone.

* * *

Once Craig and I went inside Miriam's house, I made sure he didn't stray out of my line of sight. I might not be able to wrestle an attacker to the ground like he could, but I could watch his back, so he couldn't be taken by surprise as Tony presumably had been.

Craig packed up the quilts as I finished with them, but I didn't let him take them out to the car until I was done and I could watch over him. Before long, the quilts had been tucked into two boxes and tossed into the truck's bed.

At Aaron Pohoke's office, Craig and I each carried a box inside. I left mine beside the receptionist's unoccupied desk while Crag carried his into the storage room.

Aaron came out of his office to ask me, "Do you have a minute?"

I nodded. "I hope you don't expect me to have my final report yet."

"I know it will take some time," he said as we walked down the hallway. "I couldn't look at it for a few days anyway. There's something else I need your help with. I've scheduled an appraiser to check for anything of value among Miriam's personal property, but you'd know more than he would about her quilting supplies. Do you have any idea of what they're worth?"

"There's a lot of fabric, including some full bolts, some of it designer prints that are pricey, but I wasn't paying much attention to anything except the quilts." After everything that had happened, I wasn't anxious to return to Miriam's home, but if I was going to do it, I'd just as soon get it over with quickly. "If you want, I could do a rough calculation of the value for the fabric and the more expensive supplies like batting. It would only take an hour or two. I'd need to take Craig with me, though."

"Craig left for lunch, but I can have him meet you there around 1:00 if that's okay with you."

"Perfect," I said. "I'll give you the report on the supplies when I submit the quilt inventory."

"The sooner, the better," Aaron said. "I need to get the house emptied, so we can put it on the market before the peak selling season is over."

I was anxious to finish the work too. Not just because I had other time-sensitive things to do, like finding new meeting space for the guild, but also because it felt like there was a dark cloud over Miriam's house. I wanted to be done and gone—and Craig safely away too—before anything else bad could happen there.

*　*　*

This time, Craig's truck was already in the driveway and he was leaning against it while he waited for me, finishing a bag of potato chips. He scrunched up the bag, tossed it into his truck's cab, and wiped his hands on his jeans. Fortunately, we'd both be wearing gloves while we went through the supplies, so I didn't need to worry about his getting grease on Miriam's fabric collection.

I unlocked the front door and headed straight for the sewing room, making a mental note to include the three rolls of batting in the living room, plus the quilting machine and table to my calculations. The machine was a well-respected brand, probably worth more than Miriam's car, even if Wayne Good hadn't sold her a lemon.

Craig followed with a stack of flat packing boxes. "Aaron wants me to box up whatever supplies you think are valuable."

"Depends on what your definition of 'valuable' is," I said. "The individual cuts of fabric on the shelves aren't worth much individually, but all together, they'd add up to thousands of dollars."

Craig's eyes widened. "Seriously?"

"Seriously." I could tell at a glance that the fabrics, neatly sorted by color, ranged all the way from basic and inexpensive to designer and pricey. I didn't have the time to check all the selvages for the manufacturers' labels, so the best I could do was estimate how much fabric was stacked in a single cubbyhole, and then multiply that times an average price and then times the total number of cubbies.

"Why don't you start packing the full bolts of fabric leaning against the wall?" I said, handing him a pair of disposable gloves to protect the material. "And count them for me, if you don't mind."

While I did my own calculations, Craig pulled on the gloves and began filling a large box with the bolts. He interrupted to say, "I'm going to take this one out to the truck."

"I'd be more comfortable if you'd just put them near the front door like before until I can watch your back while you're outside," I said. "I don't want someone sneaking up behind you, like what happened to Tony."

"I'm not afraid."

"Still," I said, "a good lawyer relies more on planning and precautions than on brute force. You might as well start in on those habits now."

"Okay." Craig left with the filled box, and I returned to my calculations.

When I had a total for the fabric, I turned to review the smaller supplies. There were hundreds of spools of thread, plus top-quality scissors, and several rotary cutters and rulers, but they weren't enough, either individually or as a collection, to spend my time on.

The only other items in the room that might have any significant value were the packaged rolls of batting that supplemented the bulk rolls out in the living room. They were all individually wrapped in plastic, so I wouldn't need my gloves any longer. I pulled them off and started to dig the packaged batts out from where they'd been piled underneath the worktable. The first dozen or so seemed to be specialty fibers, like wool and silk, and there were dozens of them. I didn't know exactly what they were worth, but they would be easy enough to count and then later I could do some research on the average costs.

Craig returned from carrying the third—and last—box of full bolts of fabric out to the living room. "What next?"

I nodded at the individually wrapped batting rolls. "If you'll prepare a few boxes, I'll help you fill them with the batting. I've already got all the information I need to write up the report on everything else."

"Don't you have more important things to do than pack boxes?" Craig began assembling more boxes. "It seems like a waste of your time."

"I don't mind." I grabbed the tops of two packages of batting in each hand and stood them on end inside the first assembled box. "The sooner we finish here, the happier we'll all be."

"Not me," Craig. "I was hoping there'd be time for you to tell me more about what it's like practicing law in a big city."

I knelt to dig out some more of the packaged batts. "What did you want to know?"

"I don't know," Craig said without looking up from his box assembly. "Did you ever have a Supreme Court case?"

"Not my field of law." My voice echoed in the space beneath the worktable. I tugged at the batts that were wedged into the back corner.

"Well, what about a million-dollar jury verdict?"

I'd had a few of those, but mostly what I remembered was the exhaustion I'd felt at the culmination of years and years of the monotonous discovery work that made packing boxes seem exciting. As much to remind myself as explain to him, I said, "It can be exhilarating to win a big case."

"I thought so." Craig had finished filling the box I'd started. "Champagne and caviar and stuff."

More like caffeine and take-out and hours at the computer, wrapping up the post-judgment loose ends or dealing with all the crises that had cropped up in other cases while the trial took all my attention. "Definitely stuff," I said.

"I can't wait." Craig folded down the tops of the full box. "I'm going to stop off at the bathroom after I put this box next to the front door. The door sticks in there, so if I'm not back within a few minutes, it's just because the door has stuck again, and it's taking me a while to free myself. Don't start thinking I've been knocked unconscious like the mailman."

I waved him off and grabbed what I thought were the last two batts, only to notice that there were another two behind them. Either Miriam had forgotten they were there, or she'd decided they didn't meet her quality standards. The other batts had been relatively dust-free, as if they'd been used and replaced regularly. These last two were covered with enough dust to suggest they'd been there for ten years without ever being touched. If I'd still been wearing my white cotton gloves, they'd have gotten filthy. According to the labels on the wrappers, the last two batts were generic polyester in a small size, making them inexpensive, and therefore easy for Miriam to have overlooked.

I reached for the little batts, only to find that they were heavier than the two much larger black cotton batts I'd pulled out before them. That didn't make any sense. Polyester fibers were considerably lighter than the denser cotton ones.

I rose to my feet and placed the two little batts on the worktable to inspect them. Just like all the others, these batts were rolled into cylinders and covered with a plastic bag, like a loaf of bread, complete with the same sort of plastic clip holding one end closed. I undid the clip on one and slid out the batt. After so much time rolled up, I expected the fibers to cling to each other, resisting any attempts to spread out the batt, but I didn't even have to give it the slightest push before it unrolled, revealing stacks of cash stuffed between the layers. Stacks that were about half as thick as the ones we'd found in the vault behind the framed Robbing Peter to Pay Paul quilt, but equal in number.

Apparently Miriam's financial training had never entirely left her, and she'd made sure to diversify, if not her all-cash portfolio, at least the places where she kept her assets. She must have thought that even if someone found and emptied out her vault, they'd never think to look inside her craft supplies. She'd been right too, judging by the way her living room and bedroom had been trashed, while no one had touched the sewing room.

I bundled up the batting again, leaving it and the other equally heavy package on the table, separate from the normal batts.

I was considering what to do about packing up the fabrics from the shelves when Craig returned. Compared to the cash hidden in the batting packages, the value of the fabrics was trivial, I decided. They could be left behind without much risk that they'd be stolen.

"I think we've done enough for now." I picked up the two cash-enhanced batts. "I have some other things to do, and you can pack up the fabric from the shelves another time.

Everything else can stay here for now, since there's nothing left that's likely to attract any thieves."

Craig held out his hand to take the two batts from me to carry out to the truck, but I shook my head. "I've got these."

Craig shrugged and preceded me out into the hallway. "Is there something special about them?"

"You could say that." I tossed the strap of my messenger bag over my shoulder and followed Craig out to the front door, which he propped open with one of the boxes he'd left there. I stepped out onto the porch, so I could drop the batts onto the ground near the bottom step where they'd be in clear sight while we moved the rest of Miriam's supplies out to the truck. It wouldn't take long, since Craig had backed into the driveway, so the tailgate was only about twenty feet from the porch. "They're filled with bundles of cash."

He straightened from where he'd been wrestling a box onto the porch and turned to look at me. "Seriously?"

"As serious as if I were making an opening argument," I said.

He shook his head. "I should have thought of that. Of course, you're the experienced lawyer, and I've still got a lot to learn."

Craig's eyes narrowed suddenly, focusing beyond me.

I spun to see Herb Stafford coming up the driveway with a video camera held in front of his face, pointing it at me as aggressively as if it were a weapon.

CHAPTER TWENTY

———

"Hey," Herb said from behind the video camera. "You're not supposed to be getting rid of anything until the court decides who owns it."

Craig started down the steps, obviously intent on a confrontation, but I grabbed his arm to stop him. "It's okay," I told Craig. "We're not doing anything wrong, and I don't care if Herb wastes his time recording us."

I let go of Craig, and we both continued down the steps and toward the truck, picking up the cash-filled batting bags on the way.

"We're not disposing of anything," I told Herb. "We're just putting the quilts and supplies into storage where they'll be safe from burglars. Then the court can decide who it all belongs to."

Herb peered out from behind the camera. "How do I know that's what you're doing?"

"Because she said so," Craig snapped, "and Ms. Fairchild's a lawyer. She doesn't lie."

Craig had a higher opinion of lawyers than most people did, but apparently either his confidence or his muscular build was convincing.

Herb lowered the camera and turned it off, although he didn't unbend enough to stash it in the camera bag that was hanging off his shoulder. "How do I know that's what's in the boxes?"

"Come join us at the tailgate, and you can peek inside as Craig loads everything up."

I detoured to the front of the truck to toss the two batts I was carrying through the passenger side window of the cab.

"What was that?" Herb asked suspiciously.

"Packages of batting." Fortunately, the cash was hidden in the folds of batting and the bags were transparent, showing what appeared to be nothing particularly valuable inside. I doubted Herb would ask to inspect the contents, so it should be simple to avoid any mention of the cash. "It's what goes in between the top and bottom layers of a quilt."

"What's it worth?"

At a guess, I'd say the cash amounted to about a hundred grand. Not that I was going to volunteer that information when it was simple enough to avoid the issue. "The batting for a single quilt retails for anywhere from about ten bucks to more than fifty."

Herb lost interest, as I'd hoped, and continued to the tailgate, where Craig had already tossed the first two packed boxes. "What's in them?"

"More batting and fabric," I said as Craig returned to the porch to pick up not just one, but two three-foot-square boxes stacked on top of each other. They had been among the first ones he'd packed, both filled with bolts of fabric. I would have struggled to carry just one, and he seemed totally unfazed by two. "You'll have to ask your attorney to contact Aaron Pohoke later for the value on those supplies. I haven't calculated it yet."

Herb shook his head. "No point. If Miriam's business was anything like my job, the supplies can't be worth much. Only a small fraction of the price a restaurant pays is for the ingredients. Most of the cost is in the labor."

"In theory, it should be the same with quilts." I doubted Herb would believe me, but I felt obliged to try one more time to convince him that he had unrealistic expectations about the assets he was going to court over. "In reality, though, the mark-up for hand-made items is pretty small, considering the time investment."

"You're just saying that so I'll drop my lawsuit."

I didn't need the stress of banging my head against the wall that was Herb's refusal to accept reality. Aaron Pohoke could deal with him.

I watched Craig toss the two fabric-filled boxes to the far end of the truck bed as if they held nothing more than the light polyester batts—without the cash—that I'd carried. I tried to stay fit, preferring not to add any other health issues to my syncope, but even if I spent ten hours a day at a gym, I would never have the upper body strength that Craig did. He really had been a big help with this project, completely earning his promised recommendation letter from me.

Herb peered into the box nearest the tailgate. "Where are all the quilts? That's where the real money is."

Not even close, I thought. "The quilts are already in storage."

"What about the framed one?" Herb asked. "The one on the wall?"

"That's in storage already too."

"I hope you handled that more carefully than these supplies," Herb said, pointing at the last two boxes that were tilting at somewhat haphazard angles in the truck's bed. "It's an antique, and that means it's valuable. It belonged to our grandmother. She loved it to pieces. That's what Miriam said, anyway. It was used every day, so most of it was falling apart by the time Grandma died. The framed bit was the only part that could be saved."

"I'll make a note of that for the provenance," I said.

Over on the porch, only one box remained to be carried to the truck, and Craig was closing the front door.

"There's nothing more to see here," I told Herb. "Craig's getting the last box now, and as soon as it's in the truck, we're going straight to Aaron Pohoke's office. You can follow us if you want to watch us unload it there."

Herb pulled the camera bag around from where it hung down his back and stuffed the video camera inside. "Nah. I need to talk to my lawyer. She's going to want to talk to your lawyer about what you did today."

He obviously intended his words to sound threatening, but they rang hollow. A groundless legal threat simply didn't compare to the bigger dangers I'd encountered at Miriam's house.

CHAPTER TWENTY-ONE

———

Herb took his time making sure the video camera was securely packed before he zipped up the bag and started toward the street. He walked backwards, as if he expected me to do something sneaky if he turned around.

I wouldn't feel comfortable until I knew he was really gone, so I leaned against the front of the truck to watch him leave. Craig came over to stand beside me, crossing his arms over his chest as if to show off his muscles.

"Was he right about that framed quilt?" Craig asked. "Miriam never thought it was worth much."

"I won't know for sure until I do some research." Herb was finally out of sight, so I pushed away from the bumper to go over to the passenger side.

Craig headed for the back of the truck to close the tailgate.

I was reaching for the passenger door's handle when it struck me that there was something odd about Craig's comment. It almost sounded as if he'd talked about the Robbing Peter to Pay Paul quilt with Miriam.

Had he known her before she died? Possibly even been inside her house? He had known about the sticky bathroom door, after all, and I couldn't remember him using the room before he'd warned me about it.

Craig interrupted my thoughts, calling my name. "Come look. I think maybe Herb took something. One of the boxes is open, and I know I had it completely closed."

I headed for the tailgate. "Aaron never mentioned that you'd known Miriam before she died."

"I didn't know her well," he said. "I work for the company who did her landscaping. Sometimes she'd hire me directly to do additional jobs around the place, things that were too small for my employer to be bothered with."

My stomach rolled, stopping me in my tracks. A hint of nausea followed, confirming that my nervous system was warning me I needed to do something before I passed out.

When I was first diagnosed with syncope, I'd tried ignoring the warning signs, only to regret it when I passed out. After that, I'd paid attention. Which was fortunate, since paying attention to the warning signs in situations where I shouldn't have been anxious had saved my life on more than one occasion.

Something was triggering my nervous system, and I wasn't sure what it was. I checked over my shoulder to see if Herb had returned, but there was no sign of him or any other intruder. Someone could have been crouched down on the other side of the truck, out of the line of sight for both me and Craig, and equally out of Dani's view, thanks to the shrubbery along the property line.

"I'm not feeling well," I told Craig. That much was the truth, but if Herb was nearby and listening, I didn't want to alert him to my plan to move away from Dani's blind spot and out to where I could be seen by passersby on the street. "I'm going to sit in the truck cab for a minute." From there, I could see if anyone was sneaking up on us, and call 9-1-1 at any sign of trouble that was more tangible than my nausea and dizziness.

I had just turned when Craig grabbed me from behind in what I assumed was a wrestling hold. I hadn't even had a chance to scream before he had my mouth covered and the rest of me completely immobilized. It didn't help that my nausea was in full gear and my head was spinning, although the latter could also have been because of the adrenaline that demanded more oxygen than I could get while breathing exclusively through my nose.

"I'm sorry, Keely. I really am." Craig began dragging me toward the back corner of the house. "I was hoping you wouldn't figure it out. I was really counting on your letter of recommendation. I suppose I'll just have to make do with the cash you found today. That should cover my tuition, so I don't need to worry so much about scholarships."

I managed to catch hold of the back bumper of the truck, slowing down our progress. I tried to speak through the hand covering my mouth. It came out garbled, but got Craig's attention.

"You can't talk me out of this," he said. "No matter how good a lawyer you are. There's nothing you can say that would make me let you go. As soon as you tell the cops that I killed Miriam, my life's over. It was an accident, but they'll charge me with manslaughter, and then my college admission will be revoked. Even if the school officials understand it wasn't my fault, and I get an undergraduate degree, I'd never get into law school or get admitted to the bar with a criminal record."

I shook my head vehemently and tried to say "I can help you."

He hesitated, giving me hope that he'd understood and was looking for a reason not to kill me. After a moment, he dropped the hand that had been covering my mouth, and I took in several big gulps of air to settle my lightheadedness.

"Well?" he said. "How can you help?"

After one last big breath in, which did seem to stabilize the spinning world a bit, I said, "Manslaughter charges aren't the only option if Miriam's death was an accident. I know quite a few criminal defense lawyers, and I'm sure they could convince the prosecutor not to file any charges."

"It was definitely an accident," Craig said, his regret obvious from his tone. "I never meant to hurt Miriam."

"That's what I thought," I said, leaving out my suspicion that, whatever had happened with Miriam, he had definitely meant to hurt Tony, and that was what would get him excluded from law school and admission to the bar. "Tell me what happened, so I can talk to some defense counsel for you."

"She just made me so angry that day," Craig said, leaning against the back of the truck and pulling me against him, so I was slightly off balance. "I always knew she cared more about her quilts and her piles of money than she did about people. She didn't need to be such a jerk about it, though."

I remembered what Wayne had said about Miriam's bluntness when she'd turned Herb down for a loan. "Did you ask her for money? Is that what started it?"

"I only asked for what she owed me," he said. "Or what she was going to owe me in a few minutes. I was almost done with the job, but it was going to be a couple hours before I finished. My truck was in the shop, and I needed the money she owed me to get it out, but the place was going to be closed by the time I left Miriam's, and I needed to have transportation that evening."

"So you asked her for an advance, and she turned you down."

"If she'd just said no, I'd have been okay with it. Not happy, but I'd have understood." He adjusted his grip on me, making it clear he wasn't sufficiently distracted by our conversation to give me a chance to escape. "She just lay there in her recliner, like she was some princess or something, and gave me this long lecture about being responsible and earning what we get, not expecting to have it handed to us. I wasn't like that, and she knew it. I'd been doing odd jobs for her for years, never slacking off, always doing more than the bare minimum. She knew I was responsible." He laughed. "More responsible than she was, only I didn't know it then. I never stole any money from her, and I could have. Never even overcharged her by a single minute of my time. Instead, I was always nice to her and even let her keep me here after the job was done. I let her tell me all about her latest quilts, and even acted like I was interested."

"So she made you angry, but you didn't intend to kill her."

"Exactly." Craig loosened his hold on me just a fraction, nowhere near enough for me to wriggle loose. "I just lost it. I would never have hit her or anything, but all I could think of was that after all I'd done for her, she still cared more about her stupid, ugly quilts than about me. About any human being. And I told her that."

"What did she say?"

"Nothing. I didn't give her the chance. While I was shouting at her, I picked up a stack of her quilts and threw them at her. I didn't want to hear anything more from her, so I raced out of the house. I figured she'd have tossed them onto the floor by the time I closed the door behind me." He sighed. "I should have looked to make sure, but I was so angry that I just left and slammed the door behind me."

If that had been all Craig did, it was probably a toss-up whether a prosecutor would file changes. But add in the subsequent attack on Tony and now the one on me, and the odds were that Craig would face charges for all three incidents. Not that I planned to tell him while he had me in his grasp.

"When did you realize what had happened?"

"It took me a few minutes to cool down, and then I figured I'd better finish up the job. Even if I couldn't get my truck that night, I'd need the money to get it later." Craig took a deep breath. "It was a couple hours later when the job was done, and I went to get paid. She was still lying on the recliner, the quilts on top of her, not moving. I checked, and there was no pulse."

"Why didn't you call the police then?"

"It doesn't look good, does it? I always thought I was a tough guy, but I panicked. I was afraid of what people would think, and it dawned on me that no one knew I was there. My truck wasn't in the driveway, and I'd been working in the side yard, where the neighbors couldn't have seen me. I decided to get my money and leave. It wasn't like anyone could do anything for her at that point. And I knew she had cash around the house somewhere, from the way she'd always paid me in the past."

"I'm guessing you didn't find the money."

"Who'd have thought to look behind a quilt on the wall?" he asked. "I might have looked in her sewing room if I'd had more time, but I wanted to be gone before people came home from work, or someone might notice me leaving. Probably just as well I didn't stick around. I never would have found it in the batting."

Craig released the lock he had around my neck, but kept hold of my wrist. I wasn't foolish enough to think I'd convinced him to let me go, but I refrained from struggling, since that would only alert him to my skepticism.

"Well?" he said. "What do you think? It was an accident, right?"

"I'm not a criminal defense lawyer, but if you'll let me make a call, I can see what someone with the right kind of experience thinks."

"You can't tell him my name," Craig said. "Just a hypothetical. And put it on speakerphone, so I can hear what he's saying."

With my free hand, I pulled out my phone and scrolled through my contacts, trying to find someone who would understand that I was calling for help, not for a legal opinion. I stopped at Lindsay Madison's number. The granddaughter of Dee Madison, and my ex-paralegal. There was nothing to indicate what her job was, but the name of the law firm was listed beneath her name.

She answered on the first ring. "Hi, Keely. How's my—"

I cut her off. "No time for small talk. I need a favor, fast."

"Sure," she said, her voice confused.

"Remember the Tremain case, when I got into a bit of trouble?" I said. "I've got a similar situation, and I thought you could help. I need an opinion about whether a certain set of circumstances would qualify as an accident instead of manslaughter. Could you help me with that?"

"I sort of think so." In the background, too faint for Craig to overhear from behind me, I thought I could make out the sound of a landline's buttons being pressed. Just three digits. "I'll need to call you back in a few minutes, though. Can I call you at home?"

"No," I said, hoping desperately that Lindsay was as smart and quick-witted as I'd always believed. "It'll have to be the cell phone. I'm doing some field work for Gil Torres."

"Got it," Lindsay said. "Give me five minutes. Ten, tops."

She disconnected the call, and much as I wanted to dial her right back to maintain that human contact, I had to pretend everything was fine.

"Is she good?" Craig asked as he took the phone out of my hand. He obviously didn't trust me enough to give me the chance to dial 9-1-1. "She sounded kind of uncertain. I thought lawyers always had to be confident."

"She's good." I was staking my life on it. "She's going to want to know about what happened to Tony, though."

"Tony?" Craig said. "Oh, you mean the mail carrier. I saw him leaving the police station yesterday when I was picking up some papers for Aaron. He gave me this weird look, and I knew he'd just remembered something about me. Probably saw me at Miriam's house in the morning on the day she died and didn't think anything of it until then."

"So you arranged to meet him to talk it over."

He laughed. "I didn't have to. He called me. Wanted me to turn myself in."

I was only half listening to Craig, concentrating instead on whether there might be a siren in the distance, heading in this direction. How long would it take for Lindsay to find out from Gil where I was working? And then how long would it take to convince the cops to send someone to check on me?

"Tony was right," I said. "I think you should turn yourself in too."

"Yeah, but you're trying to help." Craig used his hold on my wrist to turn and lift me onto his shoulder and then onto the tailgate of the truck.

Once I was settled, he let go of my wrist. He stayed just inches from my knees though, making it pointless to try to make a run for a more visible spot in the front yard. The one good thing about the location was that the shrubbery that hid us from Dani might also muffle the sound of the approaching police. Assuming Lindsay had indeed called them.

"Tony was trying to help too," I said.

Craig shook his head emphatically. "He wasn't. He was going to make it worse by telling my mom what I'd done. I couldn't let Tony do that to her. It would have killed her."

"She would have understood."

"I couldn't take the chance. She's sacrificed so much for me, and if I go to jail, it will all have been for nothing. I just wish I hadn't had to hurt the mail carrier. "Craig looked away for a moment and then back to me with a pleading expression. "I wouldn't have done it if it weren't for my mom. I had to protect her. It was like self-defense, right? You're allowed to kill to protect yourself or your family, right? I read that in one of Aaron's books."

"Self-defense is a well-recognized legal theory," I said, without adding that it didn't apply to Craig's situation. And then I did hear a siren. It seemed to be coming from the vicinity of the police station just a few blocks away and heading in this direction.

I still couldn't make a run for the street, but that wasn't the only way to be visible. I just had to wait for the right moment.

Craig's head turned toward the sound. Danger Cove was a quiet enough town that a siren wasn't a common occurrence. Would he realize that it was coming toward us? I needed to distract him before he did.

"Lindsay should be calling back any minute now," I said. "May I have the phone back? The sooner I answer Lindsay's call, the sooner this will all be over."

"Just don't do anything stupid," he said, handing over the phone.

"Of course not." I looked at the phone's screen as if I were truly expecting a return call, but I was really concentrating on the approach of the siren. Two sirens now, I realized. And they were approaching the entrance to the cul-de-sac. Once they turned onto this street, Craig would know he'd been tricked. It was now or never.

"Lindsay's calling," I tossed the phone toward Craig and shouted, "You answer it."

Startled, he botched the catch, giving me an extra second to pull my legs up beneath me and jump to my feet. I spun and raced for the roof of the cab, scrambling onto it and then sliding down the windshield and bouncing off the hood and onto the ground, where I landed on my butt. I heard Craig yelling for me to stop—did he seriously think I would?—and tried to get to my feet only to realize my head was spinning, and if I tried to stand, I would pass out.

The sirens had turned onto Miriam's street, but I couldn't take the chance that Craig would catch up to me and drag me back behind the truck and out of sight of the police. I couldn't risk standing, so I stayed low, crawling toward the street. Craig caught up to me about halfway down the driveway and bent down to grab me around the waist.

Even if I weren't on the verge of unconsciousness, there was no way I could wriggle out of his grip, not with his training as a wrestler. He started to drag me back along the path I'd crawled. He had me, and by passing out, I was going to make it easy for him to drag me somewhere out of sight.

How close were the police anyway? If I could just hold on long enough, it wouldn't matter if the police could see me, as long as they could hear me scream. Instead of struggling, I concentrated on taking deep breaths, hoping to delay the inevitable unconsciousness.

Craig had just gotten me back behind the house, out of sight, when I heard two sets of brakes screeching to a halt.

I took a deep breath, preparing to scream, only to have Craig drop his hand over my mouth. Still, I heard a woman's voice shouting, "Help! Over here!"

Not my voice. Dani Hudson's. It sounded as if she were standing at the fence between the two properties.

"Hurry," she shouted. "They're behind the house, on this side."

And then Fred Fields was cautiously peering around the corner, his gun pointing at Craig.

Craig knew it was over and let go of me.

Before long, Fred had Craig in handcuffs and was escorting him out front. I stayed where I was and closed my eyes, waiting for my head to clear.

I could hear voices out front—the police reading Craig his Miranda rights, Dani excitedly recounting how she'd seen me crawl into the front yard and get dragged away, and then a paramedic asking where the victim was.

Another female voice joined the background noise. "Don't just stand there," Dee snapped. "Go take care of Keely. We can't have her out of commission. Not when she still needs to find the guild a new place for our meetings."

CHAPTER TWENTY-TWO

————

Over the next few weeks, Aaron Pohoke proved himself to be an excellent attorney. He worked with the local prosecutor to see that Craig was held accountable for what he'd done. The judge hadn't signed off the deal yet, but it looked like Craig was going to plead to manslaughter and assault, with a sentencing agreement. He was never going to be a lawyer, but his prison term would be shorter than it might otherwise have been. I was cautiously hopeful that he'd do something good with the rest of his life, if only to make his mother proud of him again.

Aaron had also managed to convince Frank Dreiser to waive any interest he might have had in the cash Miriam had embezzled and the supplies and quilts purchased with the stolen money. Aaron had been able to use Dreiser's desire to leave town quickly as an inducement by explaining that if he filed a claim, the estate would drag him through the courts for as long as possible, and even if he won, the legal costs and the potential fines for labor law violations would eat up virtually all of the money.

Herb Stafford had apparently cared enough about his cousin to not want her name associated with accusations of embezzlement, so he'd accepted a modest bit of the cash, enough to pay his attorney and perhaps buy a few new pairs of jeans, in return for dropping the will contest.

With the killer clearly identified and everyone in agreement about the disposition of Miriam's assets, the museum had been able to accept the bequest without any lingering ethical concerns or worries about being blamed for her death. It had even worked out well for Miriam's neighbors, the Hudsons, since as long as the estate didn't have to prepare for a drawn-out legal battle, it had been able to settle the property line issue with the Hudsons, whose *For Sale* sign already had a *Sale Pending* sticker attached.

It really was the best-case scenario for everyone. Even the quilt guild had benefitted. In the wake of the significant contribution to the museum's general fund, Gil Torres had been able to convince the board of directors to show its gratitude to the quilting community by approving the twice-weekly use of its meeting room by the guild.

I was there for the first regular Tuesday meeting in the new location. The main project on the agenda was the preparation of Miriam's quilting supplies for sale at the guild's annual show this summer, with the proceeds to benefit the museum. Everything was laid out on the massive conference table and people were sorting the fabrics and notions into various categories and price points.

Most of the volunteers were women, but unlike the previous meeting I'd attended, there were three men today, not just one. Stefan Anderson, the owner of a local folk art gallery, was helping, although his real expertise was in the finished quilts, not the supplies. Gil had hired him to sell Miriam's collection, except for the antique Robbing Peter to Pay Paul and one other cheddar quilt that I'd chosen for them to keep as part of their collection of locally made quilts. Stefan wouldn't be able to work on the sales for a while yet, since first they had to be professionally photographed for a book on cheddar quilts to be sold in the museum's gift shop.

Matt Viera was at the meeting too, but he was deep in a conversation with Gil Torres. I could talk to him later. First, I needed to find Faith Miller, so I could get her opinion of the work I'd done on my pillow-sized quilt.

I caught her attention, and she left her spot at the sorting table to join me at a smaller table, the right size for playing cards or chatting about quilt projects. While I unpacked my carrying case, I asked, "Have you talked to Tony's cousin recently? I heard he'd been released from the hospital pretty quickly."

"Sheila was worried he'd left the hospital too soon, but he insisted he had to leave because the nurses couldn't handle all the visitors he'd received. It was really heartwarming. Absolutely everyone from his postal route came by with flowers or chocolates." Faith laughed. "Tony claimed the towering pile of chocolates was the real reason why Sheila's kids insisted on visiting him daily, not because he was their favorite uncle."

I finally got my project unpacked, and I couldn't help thinking it was wrinkly and lumpy. It looked nothing like the gorgeous picture on the front of the kit.

I handed it over to Faith and waited for her verdict while she smoothed it out on the table. She peered at a few areas I was certain were completely messed up. My stomach fluttered, and I realized I felt every bit as anxious now as I'd once been while waiting for a jury verdict.

Finally Faith nodded. "It's perfect. Or at least as perfect as any human work can be."

"You're not just saying that to keep me from giving up in disgust?" I wouldn't actually have minded having an excuse to give up quiltmaking. Although, it had been nice to sit next to Matt in the vault recently, while I sewed and he read out loud.

She laughed. "It's really not that bad. Appliqué blocks like this usually look unimpressive until they're layered and quilted. You'll see."

"I hope you're right," I said as I packed up the project again.

"I am." She glanced around before lowering her voice. "Can I ask you for a favor?"

"Sure. I owe you my future quiltmaking career, such as it is."

"It's about Miriam," Faith said. "She wasn't a bad person, and I'd rather no one else knew that she might have stolen one of my designs. I'd appreciate it if you wouldn't mention it."

"It will be our secret."

"And Gil's," she said. "I told her about my suspicions, and we talked about my buying the quilt from the museum for a reduced price, given the possible copyright issue. I thought about it, but I didn't want the constant reminder of what Miriam did, and I couldn't bring myself to destroy it. I told Gil I wasn't going to buy it, and she offered to keep that particular quilt out of the book. Miriam's reputation stays intact, and I don't have to feel like she's getting credit for a quilt I designed."

"I'm glad it worked out."

Emma approached our table. "Dee wants to know what you two are whispering about."

"Nothing she needs to worry about. Or you." I gestured at what looked like a squabble about to erupt into something more over at the sorting table, where there were quite a few sharp implements dangerously close at hand. "It looks like you're needed over there. I'll go chat with Dee while you take care of it."

Dee was at the head of the sorting table, almost lost in the huge leather seat usually occupied by the chairman of the board.

As I approached, she held out her hand in the direction of my carrying case. "Well? Let me see it."

Encouraged by Faith's judgment of the block, I pulled it out of the case and set it in front of Dee.

She nodded approvingly and handed it back to me. "So, now that you're officially a quiltmaker, what are you planning to make for the Thanksgiving parade?"

Matt came up behind me and put his arm around my shoulder. "She might not be able to finish another quilt by then. Her schedule is filling up pretty fast, between her appraisal work and now writing the text for the book on Miriam's quilts. And I've got dibs on most of her free time these days. In fact, it's time for us to be leaving."

"I'll excuse her from contributing to this year's parade, but I'll expect her to have something for the next one." Dee's eyes twinkled even more than they usually did. "I'm just surprised you two waited so long to get together."

Matt shrugged. "One of the reasons why I'm a good reporter is that I've got a lot of patience. Some stories just fall into your lap without any effort at all, but most of the time, the really good ones, they take time and persistence. Relationships are like that too."

I let Matt tug me toward the exit and waved good-bye to Dee.

Sometimes, just sometimes, things didn't always turn out worse than I'd imagined. The recent evenings in my vault, sewing and reading with Matt after dinner together, had certainly been nice, although the timing hadn't been right to see what would happen if I kissed him.

After Matt's first visit to the bank vault, it hadn't taken long for me to start thinking about all the things that could go wrong if things got serious between us. Foremost among my concerns was how he'd react to learning about my syncope diagnosis. The doctors still didn't know for sure why my system overreacted to stress, so they couldn't say whether the symptoms might worsen from their current inconvenient level to something much more debilitating.

I had to tell him about it before much longer, but I was determined not to worry about it yet. Not that I could ever completely stop thinking about what could go wrong. For now, the most optimism I could muster up was to acknowledge that the prospects for a relationship with Matt could have been worse. *Much* worse.

BOOKS BY GIN JONES

Danger Cove Mysteries
Patchwork of Death
A Christmas Quilt to Die For
Clues in Calico
"Not-So-Bright Hopes"
(short story in the Pushing Up Daisies collection)
Deadly Thanksgiving Sampler
"A Killing in the Market"
(short story in the Killer Beach Reads collection)
A Death in the Flower Garden
A Slaying in the Orchard
A Secret in the Pumpkin Patch
Two Sleuths Are Better Than One

Helen Binney Mysteries:
A Dose of Death
A Denial of Death
"A (Gingerbread) Diorama of Death" (short story in the Cozy
Christmas Shorts collection)
A Draw of Death
A Dawn of Death
A Darling of Death
A Display of Death

ABOUT THE AUTHORS

Gin Jones became a *USA Today* bestselling author after too many years of being a lawyer who specialized in ghostwriting for other lawyers. She much prefers writing fiction, since she isn't bound by boring facts and she can indulge her sense of humor without any risk of getting thrown into jail for contempt of court. In her spare time, Gin makes quilts, grows garlic, and advocates for rare disease patients.

To learn more about Gin Jones, visit her online at www.ginjones.com

Elizabeth Ashby was born and raised in Danger Cove and now uses her literary talent to tell stories about the town she knows and loves. Ms. Ashby has penned several Danger Cove Mysteries, which are published by Gemma Halliday Publishing. While she does admit to taking some poetic license in her storytelling, she loves to incorporate the real people and places of her hometown into her stories. She says anyone who visits Danger Cove is fair game for her poisoned pen, so tourists beware! When she's not writing, Ms. Ashby enjoys gardening, taking long walks along the Pacific coastline, and curling up with a hot cup of tea, her cat, Sherlock, and a thrilling novel. She is also completely fictional.

If you enjoyed this book, be sure to pick up the next
Danger Cove Mystery:

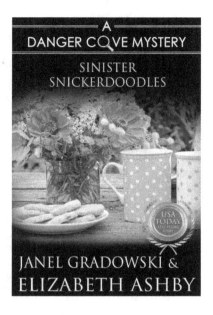

SINISTER SNICKERDOODLES
Danger Cove Mysteries book #12

Maura Monroe came to Danger Cove, Washington to forget the
past and start over. Her newly-found spontaneous side thinks
buying the Cinnamon Sugar Bakery is the perfect way to both
indulge her passion for baking and gain a fresh start. Only things
are anything but quaint when she uncovers a dead body and finds
herself smack in the middle of a small town mystery.

www.GemmaHallidayPublishing.com

CPSIA information can be obtained
at www.ICGtesting.com
Printed in the USA
LVHW111559051120
670844LV00003B/425